International Acclaim for
and
Thin Skin

"Emma Forrest has single-handedly reinvented the Hollywood novel. In prose as precise and harrowing as a knife cutting flesh, *Thin Skin* chronicles the disturbing, hysterical, genius, and heartbreaking consciousness of a young woman who has transcended her past and transformed herself into an icon for our times. A truly remarkable, hilarious, and devastating work of fiction."

—Jerry Stahl, author of *Permanent Midnight*

"Flip, shrewd, cool, sure, and insightful."

—*The Independent* (UK)

"Emma Forrest writes with the peculiar wisdom of a wicked-tongued, acutely observant young woman."

—Eve Ensler, author of *The Vagina Monologues*

"Skeletal and luminous, *Thin Skin* takes the coming-of-age novel to places it has never been before."

—Julie Burchill

"Deeply cynical and darkly funny. . . . It'll make you laugh—and think."

—*She Magazine*

By the same Author

Namedropper

Thin Skin

a novel

emma forrest

POCKET BOOKS

new york london toronto sydney singapore

An *Original* Publication of MTV Books/Pocket Books

POCKET BOOKS, a division of Simon & Schuster Inc.
1230 Avenue of the Americas, New York, NY 10020

Copyright © 2001 by Emma Forrest

Originally published in Great Britain in 2001 by Bloomsbury Publishing Plc

MTV Music Television and all related titles, logos, and characters are trademarks of MTV Networks, a division of Viacom International Inc.

ISBN: 0-7434-6481-8

First MTV Books/Pocket Books trade paperback printing February 2003

10   9   8   7   6   5   4   3   2   1

POCKET and colophon are registered trademarks of Simon & Schuster Inc.

Printed in the U.S.A.

For information regarding special discounts for bulk purchases, please contact Simon & Schuster Special Sales at 1-800-456-6798 or business@simonandschuster.com

Acknowledgments

I was encouraged to write this book by two amazing women:
Alexandra Pringle of Bloomsbury UK and my agent Felicity
Rubinstein. Jim Fitzgerald found its U.S. home—
with Jacob Hoye, who has, in his office, the same
Thelonious Monk poster as I do. Chris Potter hung my
poster and straightened out a lot of other things in my life too.
Thanks to Rachel Resnick, Bonnie Thornton, and Sarah
Bennett. Thanks also to the staff of the Chateau Marmont
where much of this book was written.

Hilary, I have so much to tell you, mostly that you
should still be alive.

"I realize I make exactly the same scream whether a great white is attacking me or there's a piece of seaweed brushing my leg."

—axl rose

Cast of Characters

Ruby *(a fuckup)*

Liev *(a lost love)*

Rachel *(a grown-up)*

Sean *(an auteur)*

Aslan *(an empty vessel)*

Sebastian *(a beauty)*

Scott *(a mistake)*

Cyrinda *(a roommate)*

Part One

One

How it ended

I muttered "Mother" under my breath, but the bartender thought I was saying "another" and brought me a fresh vodka tonic. I used to say it all the time: "Mother," "Mommy," "Mom." As a mantra, sometimes, when I couldn't think. "Quit it!" she'd giggle. "You're making me nervous." She was the only mother I know of who really giggled: "tee hee hee hee" she'd honk, like a Frenchman in a comedy skit. She was the only mother I know of who said "motherfucker"—not often, but when she did say it, listening to a politician on the radio, or surveying the poor workmanship of the man who cleaned our windows, it was with barely suppressed delight.

I lit a cigarette and looked out the window, watching the blue sky tear under the weight of pink. When the blue bounced back, it was bruised and damaged, five shades closer to black than it had been before. The keyboard whirr emanating from the practice space beneath the sidewalk offered funereal condolences on the sky's loss.

Thin Skin

Suddenly the music stopped. The grating on the sidewalk scraped, clanged, and opened. Into the semilight blinked Aslan, fumbling in his pocket for a Marlboro.

Cigarette in mouth, he looked at the stars. I stared hard at him, ten feet away, but he did not lose his concentration and he did not stop staring at the sky until the moment he took the last drag on his cigarette. Then, as if snapped out of a slumber, as though all the stars had been turned up like bright lights signaling closing time, he jolted back to life. He stubbed the Marlboro underfoot and headed back into the basement, pulling the grate closed behind him.

Without stopping to consider whether or not he wanted to see me, I paid the bill and left the bar. I didn't bother to check my reflection on the way out. If I had, I would have seen a mad woman, although I might have dismissed that as bad lighting.

I tapped on the grating but there was no response. I knelt down, the concrete kissing my knee lustlessly through the rip in my jeans. With all my might, I lifted up the grating and followed the stairs down toward the sound.

The keyboard stopped. "Who's there?" asked Aslan.

"It's me." He offered no recognition, so I added, "Ruby."

He nodded but did not reply.

"How are you doing, Aslan? Long time no see. The rest of filming went really great. I wish you could have come to the wrap party. I hear you're really good in it."

Aslan, whose name was the most nervous-sounding part of my terrified sentence, went back to playing his keyboard and I stood there feeling sick and stupid in the dark. Because there was so little light in the basement he could not see me clearly and I turned my weirdness up louder so he would know he had to help. If he heard, he didn't help. He just turned the keyboard up louder and kept playing.

I sat miserably on the bottom step and tried to will myself into another attempt at conversation. Every time I opened my mouth, I felt his dislike slap hard against my teeth. My God, I cringed, Aslan is a flower child. Aslan hates no one. He's famous for it. He loves the wind and the trees and the flowers. But the wind and the trees and the flowers are a whole lot easier to love or even to like than I am.

Finally, in a voice so quiet that the law of diminishing returns ensured it pierced the room, I threw him a question he could not ignore. "Aslan? Am I going to die?" Because I couldn't think of anything to say. Not "How's the music going?" or "What's up?" or even "I like your shirt." All I could do was sit at the foot of the stairs as the cars rolled overhead and ask again, "Am I going to die?"

"I don't care to discuss it," he sniffed.

And he packed up the keyboard, packed up the drum kit, packed up the bass that was lying on its side. When he could pack up no more, he laid the instruments in a corner of the dank room and walked past me, up the stairs and out into the world. I followed him. He turned once, to secure the grating with a padlock. And then he was gone, carried along by his anger, out of sight before I had time to break down for him.

I am going to die.

Om. Om. Om.

I am going to die.

Tonight's the night, baby.

It was only a suggestion that rose to the surface because I was trying to get a good-looking boy to pay attention to me. Although he studiously ignored me, when he stormed off, the suggestion was still there, unwilling to leave me by myself, worried about me, worried that I might do something bad.

"Do something good, Ruby. Do something to help you and everyone around you: kill yourself."

If you will hold my hand.

"I will be with you all the way."

So me and the thought of suicide walked home, arm in arm, laughing at the wind like young lovers. It was a considerable walk, but we didn't really notice how many blocks westward we were pounding, because we had so much to talk about.

"Wait there," I said, as I put my key in the door. "My landlord is very strict. I am not supposed to bring things like you home with me."

"Things like me?" huffed the thought of suicide.

"I'm sorry. I didn't mean to hurt your feelings. But you know what I mean."

"I know, I know," soothed the thought. "Let's just get on with it."

Two

How it started

I remember when Liev left. He washed his face before he did it, as if he wanted to be neat to break my heart.

I cried every day for a month. At the end of the month there were no more tears and what came out was like the bile after vomit. I struggled for air as the tearless sobs racked through my small frame. My father was impressed. It was the first truly great display of emotion I had ever shown. He had always been disappointed at how sensible I was, how calm and easy-going. As a baby I would mew rather than scream. Now I was his perfect daughter. He even sat on my bed and held me, stroked my hair and called me his "sweet, sensitive baby." I wanted to enjoy it. Although I could see his arms around me and his hands in my hair, I couldn't feel them.

It didn't help that we met there, in my parents' house. I was still living at home and he was lodging. Like my parents and me, Liev was an artist. He was considerably better than I am. His art was far more imposing and complete than mine, which seemed inevitable since he was physically so much bigger than me; his huge hand could cover my entire face. In bed, I liked to lie across his chest, like a cat, and have him stroke my hair.

Although he discouraged me from sucking my thumb as I slept, it was an old habit I had never managed to shake.

From the start, Liev had babied me. Bought me stuffed toys from the children's store, shampoo in the shape of a cat, invented a story for me about a magic bunny rabbit. I felt myself regressing, but it was so pleasant, like an afternoon nap stretched out over months. He helped me get to sleep, held me tight in the crook of his huge arm. I twirled the fur on his wrist to help myself nod off. I was so anxious back then. I was anxious about my painting, that it didn't measure up to my parents' expectations, that I could never emerge from their shadow. I would throw tantrums, convinced my work was childish, unformed, and crude.

My parents approved of the relationship. Mother took a photo of us entwined on the hammock that hung in the garden. Liev read to me as he petted my hair. After he left I lay in the hammock and couldn't read because the tears had blurred my vision. I couldn't eat because I only liked food when Liev cooked it, or when Liev undid the wrapper. I couldn't even find it in myself to tie my own shoelaces.

"Go with it, Ruby," gushed my father. "Utilize this pain. Use it to create, to start a revolution. A revolution in your heart and in your art."

My art hung on the bedroom wall, Paul Klee-esque animal daubings.

My parents had had a dinner party the night before he left. Several famous actors, artists, and musicians had attended. My father spent the evening sequestered on the porch with a Hollywood starlet. Her slip was showing at the dinner table, and so were her intentions. Mother hid herself away in the kitchen, stirring things that didn't need to be stirred and leaving well alone the things that ought to have been unsettled.

There had been a huge fuss that week because I had dyed my hair blond, by myself in Mother's bathroom. There were chunks of dark among the light where I hadn't been able to reach. My father winced every time I floated past, a cloud of angry blond. He liked to think of me as his little baby when he liked to think of me at all.

The starlet was a blond, although it was better done than mine.

Although I didn't usually drink, I tipped back two glasses of champagne in rapid succession before Liev snatched the glass from my hand. "What the hell are you doing?"

The bubbles kicked against my stomach and I named them in my head, these bubble babies. Out loud, I hissed, "You like me to be perfect, Liev, pure vestal virgin. But fuck you. I'll drink if I like."

"Don't talk like that. You don't have to talk like that to get my attention."

"Don't I? I saw you looking at her too. Why don't you both fuck her?"

"Ruby!"

The tears began to roll down my round pink cheeks.

Suddenly I breathed, "I want to go to bed. Take me to bed."

I was scooped up in his arms, a bedraggled, stinking romance heroine.

"Tuck me in, Liev."

He tucked me in. My lipstick had been wiped away. Beneath the stench of cigarettes, my hair still smelled faintly of peroxide.

I reached forward to kiss him goodnight. In a flash, my tongue was in his mouth, melting on his gums like cotton candy. For a moment his tongue met mine, a sliver of a soupçon of the tip.

"Baby," I whispered as he rested his mouth on mine. "Baby, I want to fuck."

He pulled away from me. Like lips freed from an ice cube, he felt completely refreshed and totally burned. Shivering, he walked over to the en suite bathroom. Fading into sleep, I watched him wash his face.

I slept well that night, dreaming of him. He thought of me all night too, but did not sleep. By the time I woke up, hung over but fizzy with love, he had already been gone for several hours. Discovering his absence, I waited until eleven to wake my parents. By lunchtime I had taken up residence on the windowsill, my face pressed against the glass. By afternoon I had retreated to bed. A week later I was still there.

"Daddy, oh Daddy. I thought we had so much time together. I was just getting to know him. I thought we had the rest of our lives."

I couldn't even bring myself to masturbate because I had to think of him to come.

"I'll never love again."

"Ruby," my father sighed, pushing aside a stuffed toy as he squeezed me tight, "you're twelve years old."

"But I feel it. I feel it here." I lay my hand on my pale, protruding stomach. For the rest of my life, I would wake with a start, in different men's beds, wondering where he was, with whom, and if it had all been a dream.

Three

Different men's beds

I hadn't meant to cry during sex. And I hadn't meant to go mute for the next hour while Scott shook me and begged, "What? What have I done?" And I hadn't meant to stay awake while he was sleeping. And I never planned to abandon the sleeping man who had just served his grieving wife with divorce papers. I didn't mean to make dicks hard. I just wanted to sleep in someone else's bed. I didn't want to have to wash my sheets but I didn't want to sleep on them either. I'd pretend there was nothing between Scott's legs, like a Ken doll, but then it would snake up, inflate, and get hard. I wouldn't touch it, but it would touch me.

I tiptoed out. The sleeping man had left his wife because I forced him to. But it was all a terrible case of mistaken identity. I had believed I wanted him enough to take him from her. Then as soon as I had him, I realized it was like thinking a new kind of shampoo was going to change my life. I thought of Scott less as a lover than as a hair-care product.

The night I left him, it wasn't nighttime anymore. It was the early hours of the morning, close, by my estimate, to the hour Liev must have left me. Just like me, the day I woke up to a dying mother and absent lover, the sleeping man wouldn't know what he had done wrong either.

I had gone out there to audition for a hundred-million-dollar Roman epic. Every actress in Hollywood was fixated on it because it was a great role, or they knew it was going to be a smash, or they knew they'd look cute in sandals. Big, big names deigned to take screen tests. As I walked down the hallway to the hotel suite to meet the producers, Jennifer Lopez was on her way out with her entourage, their cell phones ringing in harmony. She looked like a silent-film star and I wondered if she had ever seen a silent film or if she couldn't bear to be around quiet.

The producers told me how great I looked and I told them they looked great too. They did. It's only in fashion that the females working behind the scenes—the editors, journalists, and designers— are shockingly ugly. These women were as pretty as actresses but obviously not self-loathing enough. Even with my good face on, they saw in me the worst of what might have been if they hadn't gotten over their prepubescent dreams of stardom.

They had me read with the actor already cast as the villain. I was auditioning to be his sister and I tried, hard as I could, to make my face more like his, but I guess they just thought I was smirking because they let me go after a couple of lines.

I visited a psychic the morning of my audition who told me, "I see a future for you involving thick kohl eyeliner." She recognized me. She had read in the trade papers that I was up for the film. L.A. psychics watch the trade papers closely.

At the hotel bar that night, Scott picked me up and I let him because I knew, before he opened his mouth, that he would mean nothing to me. We went back to my room, where I threw up in the bathroom, and then went back in the living room and gave him head on the sofa. I didn't brush my teeth before I did it. I was trying to poison him. Like an idiot, he rang me the next day. And the next. He rang from his office and his Porsche and the health club and the set of the film he was producing. He offered to have me cast in his next project but I wouldn't let him. I could never have lived with myself if all those awful blow jobs were actually in exchange for something. Pretending I was poisoning him was enough for me. When I realized, too late, that he wasn't sick or dying and seemed to be getting happier and, God forbid, more moral the more time he spent with me, I had to cut him loose.

I hacked off my hair in the bathroom, as if disguising myself at the scene of a crime. I had seen pictures of his wife. She was pretty. Clearly caught between trophy wife and career woman. She had honey highlights in her hair, but I could see she was really a brunette. Her eyes were dark as marbles. I imagined her taking them out of their sockets at night and rolling them across the floor, giggling in pink silk pajamas: "tee hee hee hee."

I dyed my hair a lot that year. I was always escaping from the scene of a crime. Calling a cab from a pay phone outside Mel's 24-hour drive-in, I made it to the first plane of the new day. The other passengers in first class eyed me with curiosity and disdain.

I sat in my seat and listened to my Walkman. I felt the music coming out of me, as much as it went in. I thought about the sounds I made during sex. Sometimes I had to keep myself from laughing. I felt nothing. At worst, it hurt. At best, it was an irritation, like a fly buzzing around my head. I thought about speak-singing at the end of pop songs: "I'm crazy for you," Madonna said, dropping from her Minnie Mouse squeak to a deep, throaty purr. I said it once in bed, for my own amusement: "I'm crazy for you." Scott's breath quickened.

"God, your pussy feels so good."

And in my head, the voice whispered: "Here pussy, pussy, pussy, pussy. There's a good tabby cat."

In my haste to get away from him, I had forgotten my earrings, and though they had only cost twenty bucks, the loss made me cry. When I was little, I hated my mom leaving me so much that when she'd go out for the evening, I'd have her put a pair of her earrings through a tissue. Then I'd sit the tissue on a chair by my bed and pretend it was her. "You're a weird kid," she'd whisper as she kissed my ear, and, one hand already petting the tissue, I'd solemnly agree.

I rearranged myself in the first-class seat, trying to take the pressure off my aching crotch. Squirming, I opted to watch the movie with the sound off. It was awful. I was in it.

Four

Scott says

Oh my God, that girl knew how to fuck. I've had a lot of girls in my time, but I've never had the sexual connection that I had with Ruby, I'll tell you. The sex between us was just un-fucking-believable. It was too beautiful. I can't imagine either of us will ever have sex that great again. I always think that's why she left. Because it was too intense. She's young. She couldn't take it.

Five

To-do list

The first thing I did when I got into Manhattan was have the cab pull over at a McDonald's. I ate a Big Mac in the back, my hand lolling out of the window between bites, burger juice dripping over my rings and onto the sidewalk.

I checked into the Chelsea Hotel. I could have gone to my apartment, but I wanted to stay someplace that had someone else's dreams and nightmares in it, not my own. They gave me a good-sized suite painted mint green, less sleazy than the usual Chelsea room. I had wanted to stay there because of the sleaze, but the management overruled me. I wonder how often they do that to red-eyed waifs buckling under the weight of their carry-on luggage and failed affairs. Blinking inside walls that suggested refreshment, I washed my face and hands of dead cow. In this beautiful light, good-person's light, they felt as filthy as if I had slaughtered the beast then anointed myself with its innards. I threw up and washed myself again.

Stumbling out of the Chelsea, where a few gay boys noticed me but pretended not to, I steered my way to the East Side to buy records. Every other girl on St. Mark's Place was a mélange of piercings. I wanted to ask them if the metal was holding them together, or did it mean they were falling apart? I opened my mouth a few times to talk to my fellow young people, but they brushed past me— these people with rings through their lips brushed past ME— because they could tell I was weird.

"You're a weird kid. You're a weird kid."

As long as I bobbed my mouth open as if to speak, nobody recognized me. Film stars don't actively pursue conversation with strangers.

I went into Kim's to look at CDs. I picked up some Joy Division, Patti Smith, Gram Parsons, and Laura Nyro, then put them all down and bought what I really wanted, which was the soundtrack to *Fame*.

Purchase in hand, I drifted upstairs to videos and books, where I wandered hesitantly into the section for comic-book porn. I found one, once, under the bed of a one-night stand, and I liked it because the drawings in it seemed more human than the bloodless beings who star in porn films. I looked over a man's shoulder as he browsed a comic depicting two female roommates climbing into bed together because they were cold. He was taking too long to turn the page and I tutted impatiently. Seeing me behind him, he put it back on the rack and moved anxiously away.

I was just getting to the good part when a bunch of Goths recognized me. "Hey, aren't you Ruby?"

I replaced the comic as delicately as I could and nodded my head sheepishly. The youngest of the Goths, a fifteen-year-old girl, apple-cheeked and sweet beneath her pancake makeup, pushed to the front of the group.

"We loved the one where your father saves the world from the asteroid. You looked dope in that spacesuit. What was that film called again?"

"I like your hair extensions," I said, because I didn't want to answer the question. I knew I was the girl in the Claude Chabrol film. But no one else did. Because in the film, the one in the multi-plex, not the one in my head, I was still just the daughter. And it took so much time to be the daughter. I was in makeup for three hours every morning so I could look appropriately wholesome. They gave me a tear stick the day we shot my "father's" death scene. Nothing happened. They held it closer to my eye. Still nothing. The director stormed off the set. I tried to explain it wasn't my fault. "Hey, I'm crying twenty-three hours of the day and you just caught me on my hour off."

But by then the studio head had been screaming at him for ten minutes and he was almost in tears. So I just held the tear stick right onto my lid and I cried him and his boss a river. Then I went to hospital for the rest of the afternoon.

The boss thought I did a great job. The director, whose name the boss and I both forget, thought I did a great job. And evidently the Goths, twitching under purple eyeliner and fishnet stockings, thought I did a great job.

Six

Nap time

I had been at the Chelsea a week when my agent handed me a film the Goths could really sink their fangs into, a film that three of CAA's other young, female clients had already turned down. It was too low-budget and too sexually charged. They would have had to take pay cuts and show their tits. Since directors usually have to request that I *put my tits away,* they knew it wouldn't be a problem for me.

"Well, I suppose I might as well go meet the director."

I sighed, feigning disinterest, for fear they would take the offer back if they realized how good the screenplay was. Although it did have nudity, briefly, in a scene beneath a desk, it was the subject matter that was really contentious. The film was called *Mean People Suck.* The director, Sean, was a young man who had done well in off-Broadway theater, a Mormon from Utah. Sean had spent two years trying to get financing for his romance set during a school shooting.

"The friendless, bullied, Gothic girl takes her class hostage. She has already wounded the teacher when a handsome, popular athlete has the nerve to try to talk her into surrender. It takes all day but by the end of it they have fallen in love. By then the love is doomed because cops are outside waiting to arrest her. I like to think of it as *Romeo and Juliet* across the anger divide. Or the relationship between Ally Sheedy and Emilio Estevez in *The Breakfast Club* if it had been written post-Columbine," he'd tell potential backers, before the door bumped him on the way out.

I met Sean at a fancy hotel in SoHo, where he was noticeable a mile off among the men and women talking into cell phones as they tapped on their laptops. Sean has a face from the nineteenth century, but it's quite nice when you get used to it. At first, though, I was a little shocked. Soon his big, Victorian head was aquiver with twenty-first-century cuss words as he described the laborious process of getting his film made, and I found him less alarming. They wouldn't let us order drinks in the lobby unless we were guests, so he booked a room, even though all he ended up drinking was tomato juice. There wasn't an inch of anger in the swiftness with which he pulled out his credit card. He shrugged his shoulders as if to say, "Well, if this is what I need to do . . ."

Four to five is usually my nap time and I wasn't very coherent. When the meeting ended I asked if I could use the room he had just booked. He handed me the key. As I dozed, he rang my agents and handed me the role of the psychopathic student. By the time I awoke from my nap, plans had been drawn up at CAA for how I might tone up in time for shooting. Sean told them to forget it, saying he

wanted me just as I was. Nevertheless, as the film went into production, I did lose a little weight, because I was so excited I couldn't
eat. I took dialect classes to ditch any semblance of Brooklyn twang
and slip into a Texan drawl. I worked hard and felt happy.

It felt odd when I turned up in Page Six of the *New York Post,*
the next morning, linked to Scott. I looked at his photo, millions of
dots in gray, black, and white, and found I had trouble placing him.

Seven

The red-knuckle ride

The last night I stayed at the Chelsea, I almost died in the bathroom of Krispy Kreme donuts. I love Krispy Kremes because you don't have to chew them. You can just hold them a foot in front of your face and inhale. Your skin will be left with an oily residue, as if you have been up all night shaking and sweating from a drug with more rock 'n' roll than one deep-fried in fat.

I had done a week of filming and I was frightened. I hated handling the guns. I was getting claustrophobia from a scene shot three days in a row inside a broom closet. Sean was so kind and patient that it made me long for a tyrannical director, a screamer, a pincher. He was trusting me to know what to do, when I had so little trust in myself. That day I had met my costar for the first time, more of whom later. Suffice to say that he was so pretty and so Zen that he made me feel like a big, confused oaf. Just looking at him put the idea in my head and I was back on the bulimia bandwagon, the red-knuckle ride that leaves my index finger flaming puce.

I ate three hot donuts, then went to the bathroom and, because I couldn't lock it properly, had to do it as fast as I could. I stuck my fingers down my throat. I had, by then, developed a quasisexual method: if I thrust my fingers down my throat in short stabbing movements, I could make myself gag faster. The donut came out in heavy globs. I couldn't breathe and I felt my eyes popping.

As I bent over the bowl at Krispy Kreme, I said a little prayer for Scott's ex-wife. I hoped she was praying for me. My prayer stuttered to a halt in little clogs of blood. I didn't understand at first. Chocolate looked like blood to me when it was coming out of my mouth. Twizzlers looked like blood. So when blood came up I thought it was chocolate. They used chocolate in place of blood for *Psycho,* I reasoned. You can get away with more in black and white.

What's a Hollywood star to do when she sleeps too much during the day, when she can't listen to her favorite soundtrack all the way to the end because she doesn't have the concentration? I had emancipated myself from my dad when I was fifteen because I wanted to be able to work the long hours on the film that would surely be my breakthrough. As it turned out, it ended up going straight to video. I kept my clothes on all the way through and it was still pornographic. Everyone else in that film got their tops off, and I was the one who came out looking bad. The emancipation was set, though. I left my dad. I left Brooklyn. I left myself.

I told myself I was leaving home to advance my career, but that wasn't really true. Although I got an agent relatively easily, I would do just enough work, and no more, to pay for hotel rooms. Then I would check in and watch television all day. There's nothing like watching TV in a hotel. It's better, the way that food off someone else's plate tastes better than your own. In L.A., if I wanted to watch TV, I'd go to the Chateau Marmont. One time it was full, so I drove around downtown Hollywood and went into the first place I saw. The Magic Hotel. Down the road from the Magic Castle. It has posters of turn-of-the-century magicians on the walls. But I never got around to switching the damn TV on. I lay on the ancient mattress and stared into space. I saw myself disappearing into the posters. In the posters I could wear spangled leotards that I could never get away with in 3D. In the posters I didn't have to impress anyone, I just had to help. I was the distraction from the trick. I wasn't the faker, just the accomplice, and even then it wasn't my fault everyone was transfixed by my breasts, my smile, my feathers, and that, as they stared at me, the magician fucked them over. It made me feel better.

There was a time I enjoyed spending days by myself, buying clothes. But I gained 14 pounds in the last year and the experience became more humiliating than pleasurable. I should move to Europe because it's only in America that they have a size zero. The perfect woman, in this land of dreams, is a naught. On my last film, the costume designer gave my outfits gathers and ruffles to hide my hips and ass, and then would bitch about me before I had even left the room.

Finally I was working on a film that I could truly say fed my soul, and yet I couldn't stop eating. When I wasn't needed on the set, I would raid the snack table, then go to my trailer and throw up. I would ignore as many knocks on the door as I could reasonably get away with, and when I could ignore no more, I would answer the door with tousled hair, squinting my eyes as though woken from a nap. The Mormon director started to get nervous. I stopped throwing up just long enough to reassure him of my commitment to the project.

Under the Krispy Kreme lighting I saw that I had really nasty scars on my arms where I had cut myself the day I got to New York. My hair was growing in jagged where I'd hacked it off, and the ink in my flesh was starting to spread from the very first tattoo. And I couldn't think of any other way to hurt myself so I ate too many donuts and called it pain. It's funny. It was funny. Until I came to, choking on the bathroom floor.

I looked in the mirror. My eyes were popped, as if I had been strangled. I looked into the basin of the toilet as if a nice pair of shoes might have emerged with the puke. Or a job. Or a new direction in life. A better life. My new, better life in the toilet.

Often, I'd look at the swirling in the toilet bowl and see Freudian patterns, Jungian dreams, Rorschach tests: a butterfly, a cloud in the shape of Ireland. Other times, after red vines or cherry jam, I'd see a shark attack, the remnants when all is quiet. Pouring out of my mouth, I'd recall Robert Shaw spitting blood on a boat, his torso crushed by Jaws.

I sat on the bathroom floor and remembered that when my mother died and my father, cousins, and their respectful colleagues were in the sitting room crying in turn as a madrigal, I edged out of the room. I always wanted to be with the grown-ups. But not then. Not anymore.

I went to her room and lay in her bed. I wanted to smell her on the sheets, recall snuggleclub, when I'd press my little bottom into her tummy and she'd wrap her bangled arm around my waist. But all her bedroom smelled of was deep, deep sadness. The sadness formed a hand across my mouth, chloroform knocking me out as it had done her. I wonder about genetic predisposition to depression and mental illness. I think it happened to me because I crawled into her bed before she had left it. I could, in that moment, have stayed there forever.

Eight

Drew Barrymore or Natalie Portman?

My agent stared in disgust at the new tattoo on my wrist. He stabbed angrily at his filet mignon.

"I mean, what the fuck is that, Ruby?"

"It's Latin."

"You couldn't get a daisy or a butterfly?"

"I don't want a daisy or a butterfly. I don't want insects and weeds that are going to die on my body."

"It's not funny anymore, Ruby. It's not sexy anymore. It's not Drew. It just looks fucked up. I thought you wanted to do costume drama. There's no chance in hell we can get you a Merchant Ivory audition if you're going to keep going this way.

"You know," he added slyly, "that you can't be buried in a Jewish cemetery if you have tattoos?"

"Why are you thinking about my burial? What do you know that I don't, you filthy little kike?"

"Enough, Ruby, enough. When I took you on, you had such potential. You were so willing to work. If you had done what I said, if you had just behaved on the set and left your body alone, you would be a major star by now, instead . . ."

"I did leave my body alone. I am not in my body right now; I gave it all up. And I got to be a minor star, which is okay because it means that the ones who are really looking, who are really interested, they're the ones who see me at night."

"You're wrong. Being a minor star means that you get paid less. And that I get paid less. Honey, we could have had you in the Natalie Portman league by now."

I laid my head on the table and put my napkin over my face.

"Hmm. Natalie Portman. She seems so calm. She seems so happy. She still lives with her parents, doesn't she? Could you really make me like her? I would," I whispered dreamily, "like that a lot."

"No, I can't make you like her!" he boomed. "You're too heavy, you've got too many tattoos, and you have a horrible attitude."

"This director likes me."

"Nobody cares about this director."

"But he likes me. He thinks I'm talented. He says I'm embodying the role just as brilliantly as he knew I would."

"You're playing a school shooter!"

"A school shooter IN LOVE."

"Springtime for fucking Hitler," he muttered under his breath, then added, out loud, so loud that the other diners twitched behind their menus, "I can't work with you anymore."

I only half listened, tipping back glass after glass of red wine. Soon I was quite drunk and it was time to go home. I rolled up the sleeves of my jacket and pulled back my bangs. We both looked at my arms, him horrified, me amused. Seemingly reacting with the wine, the white lines on my arms were bubbling up, as if inflated by a children's party entertainer. "White lines," I chirped gaily. "Don't do it."

Nine

Best policy

"Ruby is the worst client I ever had."

Ten

Change of address

"This is, um, ughh—" Sean cleared his throat, his hand on my knee as he sat next to me on the sofa in my trailer. From the awkwardness with which he sat and the tiny, darting glances he kept shooting at me, one might have guessed he was going to ask if he could kiss me. Instead, he asked if I could stop being such a royal pain in the ass. Except, because he is sweet Sean, with his sweet, old-fashioned head, his doting wife and two children, he asked if I needed help.

"Um, ah, I . . . I can't pretend to know what you're going through."

"Please. Just for pretend. Just for a minute."

"Nooo." He shook his head as though he knew his reluctance to method-feel my pain was a great shortcoming. "Nooo, I can't pretend, but I can get you help if you want it. I'm pretty sure you're bulimic, aren't you?"

"I am," I answered firmly, with inappropriate good cheer.

"And I know you've been cutting yourself," he added, gathering courage.

"That too," I agreed, smoothing out my skirt.

"Well, if you know what you're doing, well, then why?"

I raised my arms up above my head and, in bringing them back down, let the backs of my fingers rest on my closed eyelids. I didn't move my hands as I answered his question: "I've started so I'll finish."

Sean closed my trailer door as quietly as he could, as if fearful of waking a beast. He let me go for the rest of the day. But when I got back to the Chelsea, he had left me a message insisting that I must, if nothing else, move out of the hotel and back to my apartment. I spent one last night in my mint-green suite. I intended to watch TV all night, but when it came to it I ended up looking out the window for most of the evening. It's hardly a lovely view: just traffic trying to get from Eighth Avenue down to Seventh, movie patrons leaving the cineplex, ripped off and grimy, bums thrusting styrofoam cups in the startled blond faces of Swedish backpackers. It's nothing to look at. But I did anyway.

I felt angry at myself for letting Sean down. He believed I could be a great actress and there I was repaying him in puke. Even a bad person can feel bad, even when in the process of being bad. But that doesn't mean they can do anything about it.

"I've started so I'll finish. I've started so I'll finish."

The next morning, I took my suitcase and hailed a cab. I asked the driver to wait until I was inside my building, implying fear of muggers, when really I was just fearful. Of my apartment being burned down, robbed, taken over by squatters.

"Can you just wait here, please driver, until I stop being so afraid of life."

It had been so long since I was home, part of me was fearful it might not even be there at all. But it was there. First the entrance door. Then the hallway. Then the stairs. Then my stairs. Then my door, which I slipped open like a burglar. Then I was inside my apartment and it was all there—all the walls, all the furniture, my bed, my belongings. The lightbulb in the bathroom that had needed changing when I left still needed changing. The milk in the fridge still needed to be thrown out. I still could not bring myself to do either.

I lay on my bed and thought about Liev.

Eleven

Way back when

Liev stayed with us for three months. Two years after he left, I lost my mother. The year after that, I left my father, a sixteenth-birthday present to myself. They dance with each other, through each other, like ghosts in a ballroom. From my vantage point at the bar, it's not always easy to tell who is who and which memory goes where.

Here is what I remember about Liev. Here's what I know to be true. I gave him his nickname. No one used it but me, which begs the question, if there is no one around to hear or share a nickname, does it still exist? Like if I said, "Hey everyone, call me 'Skip'!" would you call me that? No. No, of course not. See, that isn't being organic. That isn't playing fair.

Call me "the Boss."

Call me "Aladdin Sane."

Call me "Little Stevie Wonder."

Call me "the It Girl."

Thin Skin

Call me "the Velvet Fog."

I'm "Slim Shady."

Liev said even if it was just me who used it and my mom and dad who heard it, the nickname was still valid. Besides, he said, it was the first nickname he had ever had. It came to me the first time I met him, but at first I just volleyed about his pet name in my own head. "The Vampire." The logic of the nickname?

I called him the Vampire because he was from Eastern Europe and because his two incisor teeth rested on his lower lip, lazy and white, like Alabama trailer trash. I made Liev a button that said "The Vampire" with a kit I had been given as a birthday gift. He wore it delightedly, answering, if asked, that the Vampire was the name of a British band. He told me that one girl had said she couldn't believe she'd met someone else who was so into them: she had all their B-sides and everything.

Girls were always saying stupid things to try to start conversations with Liev. The problem was, he really didn't like to talk. His voice, which was somewhat reedy and a few notes off grating, did not fit well with his dark, brooding looks, and he knew it. I often think that my low expectations of men stem from my childhood experience of living with two vain men, and one woman who did not bother with mirrors. I'm still working out whether my mother abhorred looking at her own reflection because it upset her, or whether she simply was not interested.

Until I was ten, Mother was very beautiful. She didn't know it. She believed my father when he told her that she was not. Because she had no compact to consult, there was no proving him wrong for her. I'd try to tell her but she would hush me and say that she did not care to concern herself with such things and neither should I. But I did. I was proud, when she collected me from preschool, that my mother, with her wavy mahogany hair and dark-lashed green eyes, was noticeably so much more attractive than the other moms. I am the winner, I told myself. The next day, with the boldness of one who had just learned how to talk, I said it in front of class, during math, as I recall. Overwhelmed by the urge to share, I raised my hand.

"Yes, Ruby."

"I," I answered, rising from my seat, "am the winner."

"And why is that?"

"Because my mother is so much more beautiful than everyone else's mother."

To boos and hisses of the assembled toddlers, I was corrected.

"What?" I asked, brow furrowed. "I didn't say everyone else's mother was ugly."

The teacher, a progressive woman, shook her head. "Ruby, you are far too concerned with beauty. You must get over it if you are to function as a grown-up in the real world."

I never got over it. The world never got over it. As I got older, it became, increasingly, our prime concern, me and the world. Neither of us functioned properly, so the principal was at least half right.

When I got home, my mother had already been notified. She was appalled. She had raised me organically, in food and deed. She had me wear slacks instead of dresses. I owned nothing in pink. And yet I seemed to be turning out like a child dipped in marabou. Sitting me beside her in the kitchen, she tried, as she cut the ends of string beans, to explain why I could not go around thinking such things, let alone speaking them out loud. I did not understand. She did not understand why I did not understand.

In a matter of a few weeks she began to gain weight and she got her first gray hairs. By the time Liev moved in with us, she was fifty pounds overweight and her hair, once so wavy and gleaming, had become a Brillo brush of gray. As she chopped the ends off the string beans, her final word on the subject had been: "Please do not tell your father about this."

"Why not?"

"You know why not. It will make him angry at both of us."

That was true. My father was an ugly man, scientifically so. Though originally entranced by her beauty, he became resentful of it and sought refuge in the arms of women as painted and plucked as my mother was untouched. My father, like his girlfriends, had hair appointments once a week. The foul-smelling Fabrice would come by our house and cut my father's hair in his study. He would snip for forty-five minutes, and then my father would come downstairs looking exactly the same, although his expression was perhaps smugger even than before. My father was not a cruel man, nor a dull or stupid one. He was quite brilliant and quite foolish. As many affairs as he had, my mother put up with them all. This incensed him and led him to loathe her, for he thought she was deliberately ignoring his infidelity in order to make a fool out of him.

Liev was vain in a different way from my father. Liev's vanity was selective and well thought out and rooted more in good sense than insecurity. He chose not to talk because his voice was such that even he could not stand the sound of it. He chose not to be upset by my dubbing him the Vampire because he recognized it immediately as the huge compliment that it was intended to be. I was saying, more eloquently than all the women in his life before, that he was mysterious, handsome, and that he haunted our dreams.

"Don't call our house guest 'the Vampire.' That's not nice," said my father. "You know, don't you, that the vampire myth is rooted in anti-Semitism?"

"No, I don't know," I spat. "I'm twelve. Anyway, Liev doesn't mind, do you, Liev?"

Liev shook his angular head, responding, as he always did, silently to my father and physically to me.

"I like vampires," I added slyly. "I think that they are beautiful."

My father did not hear the lust in my praise. He did not, since it was not directed at him, hear my praise at all. I think he would be okay with incest. He could forgive the moral horror for the glory of another woman wanting him.

"Ruby, I'm not kidding: you're perpetuating a legend whose root finds itself in fear of the Eastern European coming to America and sucking the lifeblood out of the economy. A lost tribe of outcasts, wandering the earth, trying to pass as 'ordinary.' I wouldn't joke about vampires."

"I'm twelve," I told myself again, for my father was no longer listening. When his theory was finished, my usefulness was finished too, because, for my father, the point of other humans—women, children, friends, and enemies—was to listen to him be clever. And then leave. In later years, I would see other men talking the way he did. They were at industry parties, and their jaws ground like jack-hammers and they kept coming out of the bathrooms with red noses.

I didn't know what anti-Semitism meant. I knew that anti meant against. But against what? There was a lot of sex talk in our house—intellectual discussions about eroticism. Semitism sounded like it was bound to be something sexy too. I decided that people were jealous of the Jews because we were too sexy. In retrospect, thinking about Kirk Douglas and Lauren Bacall, the twelve-year-old me was probably right.

Liev was carved in the shape of sex, in the texture of sex, and anointed with its scent. I tried to pinpoint the epicenter of it all. One day, sitting in his lap, I traced the point from where it was emanating to the shiny gold Star of David around his neck. It nestled in the black chest hair that sprouted from his selection of V-neck sweaters. Although he always wore his sweaters with nothing underneath them, he never had sweat stains and he always smelled good.

The first time I got close enough to know how he smelled was at the debut of his artwork, a collection that my parents had sponsored. The "opening" was held in our front room. Liev was remarkably cool. My father was not. His biggest worry in reference to other people was not that they might be sad or nervous, but that something they might do, eat, breathe, or sleep, let alone make, would reflect badly on him. He was quite the wrong kind of man to discover new talent, and yet he had been right time and time again.

My father's mere interest in a young artist guaranteed them press coverage. He fretted in mock silence. Behind barely closed doors I heard him hiss to my mother that Liev wasn't ready for this, and that he was going to embarrass our family name. Liev heard too. His cheeks burned furious pomegranate, and, taking him by the hand, I led him into my bedroom for a game of chess. I used to be brilliant at chess. I was something of a child genius. Learning to play chess came just before the realization that learning something—anything—is mostly difficult and time consuming. Anything pre-chess, I can still do: reading, writing, doggie paddle. But I cannot do the breaststroke or mental arithmetic, because the decision was already in place. Over the years, despite pleas from my parents, the decision remained upheld.

We stayed hunched over the chessboard, as the doorbell began to ring. My mother poked her head around the door and, bowing in defeat to me, Liev followed her out of the room to be defeated by my father. Lying stretched out on my bed, I heard Daddy announce, "So here he is. This little boy I picked up on my travels in Eastern Europe. Not so little if his last girlfriend is to be believed!" Everyone laughed. I covered my face with a pillow. I gritted my teeth, fully aware that the rumor was true: Daddy and Liev had shared a lover, and that was how they met. Lila was a brilliant young artist. Daddy was going to make her a star. But then she went on vacation and fell in love with Liev. She no longer wanted to have anything to do with a self-obsessed old man, cheating on his wife and child. Daddy was so furious when she broke it off that he decided to make Liev a star instead of her.

Liev was ambitious. Lila was not. No one ever quite understood why she didn't make it, or, more to the point, why she stopped being interested in making it. Not long after Liev became friendly with my father, she moved to Philadelphia to work with unwanted children. I dreamed about joining her, my father's former lover, to see if she might want me. But then Liev moved in with us. And I decided that I wanted to stay.

I wondered about the darkness inside Liev that allowed him to leave his girlfriend, whom he knew to be more talented than he was, for the prospect of stardom, which he knew he did not especially deserve. I put the question out of my mind and, curling it tight in my hand, made a fist for the rest of the night.

As the guests followed my father into his study, Liev retreated to the kitchen. He had sold one painting—to a woman who bought whatever my father had to offer. Even if he had taken the path of his brother and lived in the East End of London selling violins, she would have bought up every one of them.

I joined him in the kitchen, perching on a stool beside him as he leaned against the table. His head was in his hands. He looked like he was crying, but there weren't any tears.

"Why aren't you crying, Liev?"

"Because I am sad."

"No, silly. I said: 'Why AREN'T you crying?' "

"Oh. I guess I aren't crying 'cause I guess I aren't sad."

"Good. Then I aren't sad with you." I leant against his chest. He smelled of fresh leather.

He bent down and put his face in my hair. "You smell of freshly laundered chickens."

"Freshly slaughtered?"

"Freshly laundered . . ." and then he started crying. "Oh Ruby, let's not talk anymore."

My mother lent Liev no comfort. By then she had retreated to her room, gray, overweight, and dejected. She was humiliated, once she began to lose them, to realize that her looks were more important to her than she thought. She forgot that she had once been interested in Liev and, though I never doubted she loved me, I could see that I made her head hurt.

They had promised Liev an umbrella of support and not only were they not coming through, they were also pretending it wasn't raining. I could not work out what there was to keep him, and I sensed, with rising alarm, that neither could he. When my father was in his study, I would crawl into bed beside my mother and nestle up close to her expanding girth. She'd put a sad, heavy arm around me and kiss the top of my head. Although her arm was now heavy enough on my back to cause me serious physical discomfort, I would not allow myself to move it until I knew she was asleep.

That year, she drifted in and out of sleep and in and out of my life.

The less my mother left her room, the more Liev and I played together. My father wavered between boredom and hostility toward Liev—his show had been, as Daddy had feared, completely derided—and relief that he was there for me to play with. Several times Liev said he felt it was time for him to move on and each time my father gave him incentive to stay, promising that they would mount another show for him. Daddy was over Lila, could barely remember what had brought any of them together. He never held grudges because he never held people in his head long enough to develop ill will toward them. His vengeance was swift and neat, then over and forgotten.

He did not want Liev to go. If he did, we would be living as a normal family and might be forced to function as such. I suspected that if Liev were not there, Daddy would have to help me come to terms with my mother's nervous breakdown, maybe even help her. Ostensibly, the lodger's purpose was to try to distract me from the disintegration of my mother. In retrospect I think I was supposed to entertain him too. And I did.

We painted together. We wrote plays. He took me to the movies. He dropped me off at summer theater camp and picked me up at the end of the day. Of course eyebrows were raised at the end-of-course meeting, which neither my mother, nor my father, nor Liev deigned to attend. And that infuriated the teachers and the other parents because they correctly suspected that Mommy, Daddy, and Liev felt there was nothing the teachers could tell them about me that they didn't already know. And if there was something—well then it was not something they cared to find out. They knew that there were directors, actors, and writers at my father's get-togethers, people who could pluck any one of them out of their day jobs at junior-high theater camp and into the big time.

If Mom, Dad, or Liev had attended, they would have learned that I was well behaved if somewhat detached. That I had no friends, but did not seem unduly concerned about it. That I did tend to linger outside the staff room during lunch hour, seeking to continue discussions that had ended in morning class. That I could not eat in the cafeteria because I hated watching other children chew, but that I snuck my lunch out onto the theater stage and crouched in a corner behind the red curtains. And that I had cried and cried when I was chosen to play Puck, not Titania. "No, no, I'm not mischievous. Fuck you, motherfuckers, how's that for gamine? I want to be the Queen because I am the Queen and if you can't see that I fear for my place in the world."

A couple of evenings after theater camp, Liev and I watched *The Breakfast Club* on tape. I liked it, despite the things I didn't understand. When I was twelve, teen films felt like a language I could read immaculately from the page, without even knowing what the words meant. Part of the reason that film appealed to me so much was that I knew I was too young for it. Liev was only twenty-five. He was young enough to miss his youth just as it was slipping away. The worst kind of loss—the one that is happening as you feel it.

Even before Mom started to leave, movies were nurture as well as nature. I saw things on the screen and saw my future. "One day I will say that line." I constructed events in my life so that I would have an excuse to repeat what had already worked for Molly Ringwald. What would Molly do? She'd say "Screw it all" and go to Paris to make a film with Godard. I lived my life so I might be lit in the style of French New Wave. Even if it meant being less happy, I wanted sad lighting because happy lighting is so ugly. Happy lighting makes me feel ashamed to be American.

"This *Breakfast Club* is European in tone," nodded Liev, putting on *Un Bout de Souffle* to prove his point. And I wondered, "Does everyone who watches French films grow into a pouting enigma?"

Yes. Of course. You learn to pout, you learn to evade questions. It seems worth it for the longest time. Until you realize how long it's been since your pouting lips were kissed by someone who didn't smell of sulphur and sour defeat.

Are people who love movies scared of real life? Yes. Of course. Everyone is. But we're brave enough to try to do something about it. Life is terrifying and we will seek not to cross uncharted territory by never saying anything that has not already been said by someone more beautiful, someone more dead. Someone who had their back teeth removed so their cheeks might appear more sculpted on screen. Now *that's* entertainment.

"She's a perfectly awful little girl," I overheard someone say at one of our dinner parties, "spoiled rotten," which made me laugh as hard as I cry because, as Liev said with indignation, "Who is there here to spoil you?" He got angrier and angrier. "Children *should* be spoiled. Little girls and boys, babies should be spoiled rotten, until their ears grow weary of constant demonstrations and declarations of love and adoration. That's how it works where I come from."

Since I was schooled at home, I didn't really have the opportunity to play with little kids, to wear Band-Aids over grazes and pin the stupid tail on the stupid fucking donkey. I never had a chance to give head to a grateful teenage boy. By the time I met men that way, by the time they were passed to me, they weren't grateful at all. They were spiteful about the sex act, expected me to be grateful that they deigned to put their dicks in my mouth.

My parents thought that school would stifle my freedom and natural curiosity. They took me out of preschool because I was reprimanded for a drawing I had done of a park. Ripping up my paper, the teacher scoffed that the sky wasn't green and the trees weren't blue. It's like they were trying to keep that from me. My parents were furious. They said that my art had gone over the teacher's head. From that day on, I stayed at home. My mother taught me how to read and how to write. Then she taught me how to stare, absentminded, out of windows, at nothing. It wasn't until quite recently that I figured out what we were staring at. The last Russian doll after the smallest one has been revealed: the one so tiny that there is nothing there at all.

Liev has always meant so much to me because young girls remember the first person who tells them they are beautiful. The first person who isn't your parents. My father didn't say it. I think my mother didn't say it because, after the I'm-the-winner incident, she didn't want it to shape my notion of myself: that I ought to be beautiful. Liev thought I ought not to be so beautiful. He said it would have made things easier. I believed everything he said and for three months I was a glorious knot of arrogance, my preteen body tight with pride, I all but bounced off the walls. I wonder what would have happened if I hadn't been so beautiful, so fresh and clean stepping out of the bath that night, if he hadn't been the one to catch me in his arms and wrap me in the towel? He might not have wondered, alone at night after putting me to bed, appalled at himself, dreaming of holding the towel again, until I couldn't bear it any longer and took things into my own clammy hands, dry champagne in my belly.

But of course it was him. In the preceding weeks it had only been him, more than ever. Before Liev existed in my life it wasn't really as if my parents were there in his place, dominating my world. I did not look to them for help or understanding. They did not give it to me. Neither did they give me any unkindness or cruelty. We were all just in a different movie, my mother, my father, and me.

My father, briefly, found life in Lila. My mother embraced, with the passion and tenderness of an ingenue, the slow death of life alone in bed. I found life in Liev. He found life in me. One of us thought very bad things, something we could go to jail for. One of us thought something the world could never ever understand, but excused because of youth, because they could not bring themselves to believe that the very young could want such a thing.

The world cannot bring itself to believe that the very young can want. Like that. With full tummies and eyes half closed.

The physical image, which my mother had so often encouraged me to pretend did not matter, *did* matter. It may have been her greatest failing as a parent. Things would have been very different if it weren't for the distance between my eyes and the fullness of my mouth. In time my eyes would move closer together and my lips lose their cushioning, like air from an inflatable sofa.

If I hadn't been so beautiful, I wonder if he might not have left. After he did leave, after he stopped writing cards and we never heard from him again, that's when I started to wish I were ugly. But it wasn't until after my mother died, and I legally emancipated myself from my father, that I started putting my wish into action.

Twelve

Out of cash

I was lying in bed, dropping ash on myself, crying because I didn't have enough money for a new roll of toilet paper. I had just spent $60 on Percocet and another $50 on a bunch of quaaludes. My drug dealer surveyed the room, littered with new clothes I hadn't even taken out of their wrapping, clothes I hadn't even liked when I unhooked them from the boutique rod and dropped them at the register. Items I felt such indifference toward that I hadn't bothered to pretend to the salesgirl that I wasn't going to treat them like shit.

Strapless sequined tops labeled "dry clean only," peach suede hipster pants, a gossamer bra that tied at the front with electric blue ribbon. No one could wear such a bra under clothes, because it bulged and bulked beneath the fabric. And it didn't look good by itself either, anathema to the contours and curves of my body, which oozed above and beneath the cups like Play-Doh. The only place that bra looked good was on the floor. I had pulled up the carpeting because I felt the shiny wood surface better framed the clothes I dumped there.

Labels, label, labels, which I ripped from the necks of my purchases because I knew how pointless that rendered them. I'd pick fights with the frightened outfits. Ha ha ha, you're stupider than me: a Prada sweater with no Prada label in it, castrated cashmere. I tortured my clothes thus, as though plucking limbs from a daddy longlegs. You used to be a high-priced Helmut Lang dress? Well, you're mine now, bitch.

Halston, Gucci . . . Fiorucci! It was a Sister Sledge reunion passing unnoticed on my bedroom floor. And me, barely more noticeable, under dirty sheets, with smeared mascara and a toothache. "Oh look, wow! She's the saddest junkie!" I sang zestfully to myself between sobs. My drug dealer looked around the room and decided that he couldn't let me go on like this. So he called up the deli and had them deliver toilet paper.

"A four-pack," he said grandly, "of extra soft," putting his arm around my shoulder.

John doesn't take drugs at all. He doesn't drink or even smoke. He's doing this to put himself through med school.

"John," I wailed. "I've got a headache. I mean a toothache. And I hate my knees touching. I hate the feel of my hair falling on my face. My eyelashes are scratchy. I . . . I . . . my life hurts."

People of an especially tough disposition are often described as being "thick-skinned." I think I am a skin too thin. I cannot be here now. I cannot Be Here Now. While I'm on the phone to someone, crying, I'm always flicking through my address book and trying to get off the phone so I can ring someone else and cry all over again. I always stall on C. Sebastian Chase: home number, home address, work number, fax number, number at mother's, address at mother's, e-mail, and cell. I'm waiting for the day when I realize purely by chance that all of Sebastian's numbers are out of date and I didn't know because I haven't used them in so long, or even stopped to look at them. I started to cry, but John didn't notice because I hadn't stopped.

I know in my head where the tears start and stop. Liev would know, by instinct. Sebastian learned to figure it out, after I promised not to talk about Liev or my childhood, my father and my mother, not to talk about Brooklyn anymore. Sebastian tried so hard, so fucking hard. If he didn't want to hear about Liev, then I would just talk about Liev to myself. Sebastian tried to help, as best someone who was there to work for me could help. He did well. You have to really understand me to decode the flood of tears that supplanted recognizable emotion a long, long, *American Pie* time ago. He didn't understand. But he tried. Happy tears? Sad tears? Pain tears? Sebastian would tilt his head, tilt my head, touch the tears, lick them and respond accordingly.

"Baby's got nothing to be frightened of" or "Baby shouldn't keep getting tattoos if they're going to itch her all night."

He was right. I can take the pain. Easily. I just can't take the itching. I have no pain volume control. "A mosquito stung me! Dear God, put me out of my misery!" I can put needles and knives in myself, but I am horrified by an itch on my foot, or by my period, which brings wild terror to my eyes because I never invited it and it's not just in my house, it's in my body. My period never feels like a visitor from nature. It feels like sexual harassment.

I like the cuts—they comfort me—I can't lie. My thoughts are messy, my emotions are messy, my body goes in and out at will. The raised white scars on my arms and legs are the only aspect of my being that come close to minimalism. They came from chaos, but it is hard to carve frustration and unease into the flesh. Only straight lines. Every fear, every night terror, every hour I cried for Liev, every fight with Sebastian is registered as a neat white scar. The tattoos came because, as angry as I was, I was also tired.

Every now and then I'll be so sad and so lazy that I'll pay someone to interpret it all in needle and ink. "Do what you like," I say, because the eventual pattern is irrelevant. I just want to feel the needle and see, next day, next week, forever, the reminder that it really happened, that I really was that sad. Because when I'm on the upswing, manic as anything, I can't imagine that I will ever come down.

The samurai must always think of death. I will die of sadness, on a bicycle cycling through Tuscan hills, or in the checkout line at Kmart. But I will not be afraid.

Everyone asks how I'll feel about the tattoos and scars in thirty years. I always say: "I'll like them." I've always loved damaged monuments, in architecture and in humans. I like Brigitte Bardot now, petting stray dogs and sitting in the sun, skin getting more and more leathery. I was trying to be a ruined beauty then, at twenty. I wanted to know how ugly I could get, how ruined and ugly and spoiled, before they stopped trying to fuck me. I didn't think they'd ever notice. Nobody had so far. Because I was still in the shape of a beautiful girl. Although I behaved like an ugly one.

Even with my arms covered so you couldn't see the scars, the high-maintenance hair color told everyone on the set of *Mean People Suck* that I was damaged, demanding, fragile, and fake. They only had to put a prop in my hand, to fit me for a costume, or hand me my morning coffee, to see that. On a bright morning, as all mornings on the set invariably were, the blue of the sky bounced off the white of my hair in such a way that you couldn't really see me at all. I was the girl beneath the hair and the sky. I started to look forward to long interior shoots, three days in a classroom, in a broom closet. I loathed the exteriors.

It was Sunday morning, my first break in a while, and I was hanging out with my dealer, who soon left, having installed the new toilet roll in my gray marbled bathroom. I swallowed a Percocet and started to feel better. Drawing back the blinds, inch by inch, I surveyed New York Street Scene No. 1: another glare day, when people scrunch their pretty faces ugly in the sun.

"I can't die," I reminded myself, "because tonight I have to be in Brooklyn, where the dining room will stink of cats and Grandma Yetty will again note how much weight I've lost since I stopped seeing Sebastian." Grandma Yetty is a grandma, but not mine. She used to babysit me when I was a little girl.

When I first told Grandma Yetty I was seeing Sebastian I said he had an English literature degree from Harvard. Then I told her that he was black.

"White-black, I presume?"

"What are you talking about?"

"You know, like a white South African. As opposed to a black South African. Is he a white-black?"

"No. I don't think there are any white-blacks, Yetty."

"Oh," she said dejectedly, "well, is he black-Jewish?" Her voice grew more hopeful: "Like Sammy Davis."

"No. He's not like Sammy Davis. Um. At all."

My mom, I remember, believed in intermarriage. She told me such things from the time I was tiny. Perhaps she was trying to cram in as much as possible, whether or not it was appropriate for a little kid, whether I asked or not, because she knew she wouldn't be here when it was appropriate. When I was seven I asked her how babies were made. She told me, truthfully, zestfully, as though reciting a wonderful family story she had been aching to repeat. Then she asked if there was anything else I wanted to know. I asked her, "How do lesbians have sex?" And this she told me unabashedly too. "Sex toys" were mentioned as an option and from that day forth I associated lesbianism with theme parks and petting zoos, somewhere fun to visit for a day.

I remembered very clearly that she thought Jews and blacks were a great combination. "Marry out, marry out!" she directed one evening, as she scrubbed me in the bathtub, rubbing soap behind my five-year-old ears.

I loved Sebastian and I loved going to his mother's house in Jersey. I loved traversing the boardwalk, in the wrong shoes at first, but they became righter and righter the more I walked. After we broke up and he broke down and I broke in two, I would go back and walk. Maybe I was hoping to bump into him. No. I was hoping to bump into his mother. I wanted to tell on him and tell on myself. I did a bad thing, Mrs. Chase. I'm a bad person, Mrs. Chase. Okay, I'm not. I'm glad you said that. It means a lot. Yeah. He's okay. He's seeing other people, Mrs. Chase. Oh, he hasn't told you about them? Then I guess they don't mean that much, these new girls.

I rode the train to Jersey, to the boardwalk, but I never saw him and I never saw her. I just saw myself. In the sea, in the shopfronts. I saw myself reflected in things that don't reflect. The wood beneath me, the splinters in my soles bore my face. Discomfort is worse than a wound. At least you know where you are with blood. At least other people can see it.

"You're looking thin," said Yetty last time I saw her. I really wasn't, but I deserved to be: for those last few months, all that I'd lived on was blow jobs and cigarettes. If it had worked for me as it had every other heartbroken girl in New York City, I would have turned my diet into a book and topped the bestseller lists. Yes, you too can achieve your target weight in less than a month, or your money back.

Don't look at fat dead Mom. Or cold living Dad. It's not my family's fault I've had such a bumpy ride. Yes, I've cried and cried because my mother is dead and because she did it all by herself, without the aid of cancer or heart disease. But still, I have never cried as hard as when Liev left. Or as hard as I did when I knew he was not coming back.

After Mom was gone, I started to hate Dad less. He became so tiny and ridiculous. And then, as soon as I emancipated myself from him, he no longer had to feign the slightest interest in me and, once that happened, he began to find me a more intriguing proposition. He would actually ask me what I thought of his latest exhibition or protégée. I would tell him and then leave, because I did not like being around him as he began to humble. When he started to care, I could barely tolerate him or his house or neighborhood.

It is worth visiting Brooklyn to see Manhattan. It's worth living in hell to get a better view of heaven. That's stupid. Brooklyn isn't hell. It's just where my family comes from. Manhattan is where I made myself. Los Angeles is where they took me because they liked what I had made. Manhattan is where I returned to be disassembled. Smiling and fresh-faced, unaware of imminent implosion, I bought a Greenwich Village apartment, and met Sebastian the same week. By the time we broke up, I barely knew my own neighborhood. So I went back to L.A., to auditions, to Scott, to quasiauditions and quasi-Scotts.

Working on *Mean People Suck* I was forced to reacquaint myself with my lovely apartment on its beautiful block. I hated it.

"Excuse me. Where is the mailbox?" I'd ask, only to be told that it was on the corner of my street. I'd go and try to mail a letter to an ex-lover in L.A., but I'd get distracted and end up leaning on the mailbox until a teenage girl asked me, "Are you her, or do you just look like her?" I couldn't answer myself. That's when I first met the kids next door.

The kids next door are twin sisters from Queens. One twin has red hair and one is blond. They told me their names over and over, without malice, or offense taken, but it took me a while to process. I noticed, in order of recognition, that both sisters are snappy dressers, heavily accented, fun, smart, and very kind. When I realized how central the last attribute was to their outlook, I felt ashamed that I had been so bowled over by their clothes.

They were the first girls I knew of to wear pants under a skirt. They never wear makeup, unless they are bored, and then, contrary to the belief that makeup should enhance your beauty, they paint a green strip above each eye or add a dash of hot-pink blush until they look like punk-rock dollies.

A red twin found me sitting on a bench outside the nail salon, waiting for my nails to dry. I had been there an hour, staring at the tiny pink heart painted in the upper right corner of each nail.

Do my nails love me? Do I have a heart beating under each finger, each with the ability to function alone from the rest of me? I wanted to be alone from the rest of me, too. From the hair that fell on my face, and the knees touching each other, the scratchy eyelashes and toothache. From the certainty that I was failing Sean and that if I wasn't failing him, he was surely failing me.

"Hey, movie star," boomed the red twin. "You've been there all day."

She knew because she had been watching from her window, as she bathed a dog in a tub filled with Kiehl's vanilla cleanser. I couldn't really talk. I could just about hear. Hers was a new accent and I liked it right away. Liev's nonspecifically other accent was still my favorite, although Sebastian's drawl came a near second.

She insisted I come up to her apartment for peppermint tea. It was her apartment because it was in her name, but her boyfriend had all his records stored in the living room and her sister regularly ran up phone bills totaling hundreds of dollars. A thoroughly unexpected ferret slouched across the floor, arrogant and shifty, and a baby alligator had meek occupation of the bathroom sink.

I sat on the sofa and petted her teacup Chihuahua, which was still a little wet and smelled of Kiehl's. Its short hairs dotted my freshly painted nails. As I drank a few sips from the cracked mug, the red twin kept disappearing and coming back flustered. I thought she was taking coke, and I thought it sucked that she was sharing her stinking peppermint tea but not her drugs. The red twin later told me that she kept running to the back bedroom to try and wake her napping boyfriend.

"Guess who's in the front room. You have to get up or you'll kick yourself."

"Is it Led Zeppelin?" he enquired, raising his head of curls from the pillow.

"No," she answered, frustrated, and he went right back to sleep. Once Arlo and I did start hanging out, he still didn't know who I was. He introduced me to the drummer in his band with great excitement. "Guess who this is! It's Ruby. She's famous. She was in that show *My New Robot*! You know? From when we were kids? The one about a little girl whose best friend is an android."

"What the hell is *My New Robot*?" I asked, perplexed.

We determined it to be a sitcom he had dreamed. Jesus, I could pitch *My New Robot* to my former agent and he'd probably think it was a great vehicle for my talents.

My talents are: I knew what I wanted. I knew what I didn't want. I knew at a young age. I had big breasts at a young age. I have a round white face like the surface of the moon. It looks fat in real life but girlish on film. I carved myself an unforeseen niche as the fucked-up girl for any kid who thinks they are remotely interesting or unusual to have a crush on. The people who like that really like it. I have the added advantage of scrubbing up nicely when I feel like it, so I look like I have range, when really I just have good skin.

The red twin and the yellow twin, their boyfriends, puppies, and ferrets distracted me from the worst of the drugs. We smoked pot now and then and laughed at the animals. Sometimes I'd go on my Percocet benders, but that was it. The kids next door had never met Sebastian Chase, but I regaled them with enough stories that now whenever I mention him the yellow twin spits, "I hate that asshole." "I hate him."

I had reinvented Sebastian for those who weren't present in my life before he left it, and I was damned if I knew what was true or not. He must have done something to make me send him away. I never told them about how he knew which tear was which. It didn't seem like such an engaging story. I didn't want to hand it out as we fed the ferret or washed the puppy. I'd been thinking about Sebastian for a couple of days. I thought about how nice his body was. Then I thought about how, when you really really think about it, sex is a pretty weird thing.

Then I started thinking that blow jobs are especially weird. Then I thought about it so much that, for a whole day, I convinced myself there was a cock in my mouth that no one else could see. I thought about it some more, and then I was leaning over the toilet bowl, heaving up my guts. "Please don't let there be a cock in my mouth, please don't let there be a cock in my mouth," I was weeping when John arrived at my door that afternoon. He pulled me just about together with a couple of Xanax. I got to work the next morning.

I had to owe him the cash. Even though my previous film did great business, I still needed money. I don't know where it goes. I have a grand and then the day ends and I have nothing to show for it, except bits of string, maybe some chewing gum wrappers.

I missed getting to look at Sebastian. I missed watching his abs flex with each breath he drew. I missed the way his long lashes curled at right angles. I missed the way the clean lines of his body made me feel clean, redeemed just because I was with him. It seemed so preposterous to me when cabs wouldn't stop for him. Everyone should stop for Sebastian.

Is it okay to like someone just because they are beautiful? Yes. They make us feel less alone. I like beautiful people the same way others love sports. It is a definite answer for those of us who don't understand mathematics. In beauty as in sports and math, there is right and wrong. There is a winner. Whereas art and music are open to interpretation and people are still arguing about whether or not Bob Dylan is as significant a poet as William Blake.

The answer is they both lose because they are both ugly. Jakob Dylan is the winner. And Blake is the runner-up because he's dead so no one cares what he looks like. You see where my mother comes in? That's how she saved herself. Why is Audrey Hepburn a saint? Because she was beautiful or because she is dead? Both. It's the best way to be. Did the woman who leaped to her death from a Lower East Side high-rise last week feel less pain than Marilyn Monroe? Or did she not have hair like cotton candy and a face with all the airy sweetness of angel food cake? You know the answer. You know as well as I do that if you're going to kill yourself, you'd better be beautiful or everyone will think you were just being a whiner.

Liev wasn't beautiful. He wasn't yes or no. He was confusing. If he was yes, or even no, I might have gotten over him. I spent so many years mourning Liev—years when I could have been meeting boys, going dancing, smoking illicit cigarettes. It was only when I emancipated myself from my dad that I kind of emancipated myself from Liev too. If he did not want to come back or be with me, or even get in contact, then I decided he was no longer alive.

The time came when I decided to declare him officially dead. Like a kid seeing off an expired hamster, I took his photo into the back garden of our house in Brooklyn and buried it a foot beneath the earth. I stuck a little cross in the reshifted earth, which failed him on both levels—that we were Jewish and that I still dreamed him a vampire. Rest uneasy, Liev. If you choose not to return to me, then do not rest at all. I think it backfired, because my life since then, since the day I buried my first love in the backyard, has been tumultuous and lonely. Maybe I am now the vampire. I went out and found myself an agent that day.

In the back of my mind, the mind that I had left, somewhere under the earth with his picture, I never stopped wondering what became of him. The last postcard we received was postmarked Paris. I remember being incensed that it was addressed to the whole family. I suppose if I really did love him, if I thought there was any realistic chance that we could forge an adult relationship, I would have gone to France as soon as the emancipation documents came through. But I didn't. I never even went to Europe. In fact, when it came to press tours I actively avoided it. I'm notorious within the business for my refusal to promote the product overseas. I was sure that if I could just fall in love, really in love, rather than the smug— *Hey, everyone, I have a boyfriend*—emotions I felt when I was living with Sebastian Chase, I might be able to banish the vampire from my thoughts for good. Twins of many hues, drugs of different shapes and sizes, and all the unexpected ferrets in the world couldn't distract me from that.

Thirteen

Why Sebastian should have been happy I dumped him

"I want to kill myself," I said as I dragged kohl across my heavy lids. "I want to kill a baby. I want to die from an abortion."

Sebastian pulled a white T-shirt over his six-foot-three-inch frame, his broad shoulders stretching the fabric. Speaking through his teeth, which he did when he was tired, he replied, "I want an ice cream."

My brown eyes narrowed to black as I considered his request. "Okay, then."

I stomped behind him as he skated to the Polish 24-hour diner on the corner of 7th Street. "Christ, Ruby, I feel like I should request a child's booster seat for you," he said as I bounced around my chair, fizzing from the sugar in the chocolate-flavored chocolate syrup. Grinning, I dribbled it down my chin.

"Ruby, that might be erotic if it were strawberries."

I smeared it across the whole lower half of my face until I was wearing a sticky chocolate beard. How ugly can I get . . . how ugly, before he cannot look at me?

"It's not working," said Sebastian wearily, for we had been through this many times. "I'm not going to stop liking you."

Defeated, I tossed my maraschino cherry at him. He deftly caught it, folded it into a napkin, placed it in an ashtray and went on with his sundae, picking around the nuts. He rethought his words, upgrading them like a last-minute hustler at the Virgin Atlantic check-in desk.

"I'm not going to stop liking you. I'm not going to stop loving you."

But then he did.

Fourteen

Compare and contrast

I loved her. I really loved her. I still do. But all that kicking in her sleep, all the crying and talking about the vampire. It was hard. I've had a lot of girlfriends. I've had girlfriends before who had eating problems, anorexia or what not. I wish she had taken better care of herself. All my girlfriends before her, even the anorexic ones, they always exercised. I was at college running track. Most of the girls I met were running track too. They were pretty buff, tough girls. Some of them would get fucked-up on coke and start bawling. But none of them, even the anorexics, were fragile like Ruby was. I guess like Ruby still is.

Just 'cause I've stopped seeing her doesn't mean she's ceased to exist. I care about her. I just can't have her in my life. I guess she's driving some other poor schmo crazy. I guess I did feel, at times, that I could be anyone. It was kind of like Ruby going around town shouting, "Hey, everybody, look at the size of this black guy I caught." I think she really hated herself for liking me because I'm black. Ruby's family is really fuckin' racist. They say they're so liberal, but they always wanted her to be with a Jew. That's why she secretly loves being a movie star and loves Hollywood. 'Cause everyone knows that it's all run by Jews, and that's not anti-Semitic, it's just the truth. I think she feels she's doing her family right.

She was always telling people how tall I was, how beautiful I was, how well built.

She wanted me to fight all the time. We'd be at a party and she'd press her face into my chest and say, "Him over there! He tried to make me dance with him, and when I wouldn't, he said I was ugly!"

Nobody said she was ugly. Except her. But I'd have to step up, and we got escorted out of a few parties I was really excited to be at. When we were in front of other people, whenever we were in a crowd, she wanted to be protected. But when we got home, and it was just us, she wouldn't let me help her. It was like the guy trying to prove that he's heterosexual by making out all over his girl in public and then not touching her in the cab afterward. She wanted everyone to see that she needed help. And it made people not want to help her. I was the only one. And she screwed with my heart. Intricate little screws in my heart, tiny and sharp, nailed tight while I was sleeping, until my heart was screwed so close to my lung I couldn't breathe right.

She would get drunk and start telling everyone in the bar about the size of my dick. It was humiliating. I know on paper it shouldn't be: "Oh God, I'm so upset because my girlfriend's telling everyone I'm hung like a donkey." But it was fucking humiliating. I'm not like that. I don't talk about things like that. I mean, I'll talk about it in the bedroom, if it's me and some girl. But I didn't even want to talk about it to her. I didn't like talking dirty with Ruby because, I told you already, I really, truly loved her.

I tried to tell her she was making her life crazier than it needed to be. That nobody ruled her. That nobody said she had to slash her arms and leave ten minutes into any meal to throw up in the john. I tried to tell her that she wasn't going to become who she thought she was by reading biographies of people she thinks are geniuses. I tried to tell her that I wasn't a shiny, happy person myself but that she made me feel less alone. And that if she felt the same, then we were in love.

She didn't feel the same.

Fifteen

I love you fuck off

Yes, I heard him going around town saying how much he loved me, but that doesn't matter one iota because he couldn't help me. I was begging him to help but he couldn't understand. He thought help was going down on me. He thought that made me happy, made me saner with each lick. The only part I liked was being fucked, no orgasm in sight, just something huge inside of me, filling out the spaces coveted by demons. I tried to get him to smash me, so that the demons would be smashed too. But he wanted to be nice and slow and please me. He didn't understand.

I would try not to be sad, but I couldn't help it. And it wasn't long before his concern turned to frustration and then to disdain. "For Christ's sake, Ruby, cheer the fuck up." I heard it as "Cheer the fuckup!"

I pictured myself being encouraged from the sidelines of the foot-ball field by a squadron of tan blond girls: "Two-four-six-eight, who do we appreciate? Breakdown girl! Breakdown girl! Go! Go! Go!" And so I behaved like even more of a fuckup, because the girls in my head wanted it so much. When I slumped over the dinner table, head in hands, Sebastian would say, "Stop acting out!" It was a phrase he had heard from my therapist in a session he attended with me, and he put it to good use.

I wonder, sometimes, if I might have stayed afloat longer if I hadn't been with a man who had so very few problems of his own. The only problem he admitted to was me.

"You know, Ruby," he threatened after a fight one night, "I don't know that it's such a good idea for me to be seen out with you. You're too volatile. It's not good for someone in my line of work."

"Bullshit. You're a personal assistant. How many personal assistants actually get to date the movie stars they work for?"

"And how many movie stars are being put off from hiring me because of my association with you?"

"You motherfucker." His mother was beautiful. She loved him. He should fuck her.

"Oh come on. You don't do the premieres. You don't cooperate with the press. You're not putting yourself out there, unless it's some awful, tabloid shot of you shoveling donuts in your mouth."

"You said you liked my body. I thought you liked me this way?"

"I do like your body. You're just so unhealthy. It's disgusting." He calmed down. His voice lowered as he tried to say, as nicely as he could, that he could help me formulate a better diet. "If you just had a plate of steamed vegetables every day instead of all that greasy carbohydrate and empty sugar calories . . ."

"Oh, fuck you."

"Oh, fuck him!" yelled the red twin, incandescent with rage. I remember telling the yellow twin, whose mind I had polluted against him, that I might go back with Sebastian.

"You won't," she snapped, "because he won't let you."

"But," I reasoned, "the last time I saw him, we were walking through SoHo, looking at shops and holding hands."

"That doesn't mean anything," she sneered, clutching a ferret to her voluminous bosom, "and stop holding his hand."

I stared out the apartment window, as my mother had taught me to, and murmured, "I liked him. I liked him because he was so quiet."

The yellow twin snorted her disgust. "Well, he's obviously going to be even quieter in your life from now on."

Sixteen

PA

The studio head first assigned him to me. I didn't ask for an assistant but in the end he was very helpful. Right away, I wanted to be his girlfriend. I wasn't sure that I could love him, or he me, but if ever there was good boyfriend material it was him. He was so clean, so healthy, I wanted to lick his skin. The educated black man with the good-money job and the skateboard. Sebastian with the trim stomach and neat dreadlocks. Sebastian with the good heart and wicked vocabulary.

I drifted home, dreaming of ways to torture him, schemes to get him to buy me things. John came over and I took a Percocet and watched David Letterman. When I fell asleep, my subconscious took over, and I dreamed I was strong.

Sebastian Chase rang a few times, but I said I was busy. I wasn't. I'd let the phone ring and ring, desperate to pick up, desperate for help. I'd try to pick up the receiver, but the phone would go numb in my fingers and drop to the floor. I could not leave my bed. John went away to Jamaica for a week on research and there was no one to administer relief and nothing for me to do.

My body shook. My chest and stomach broke out in tiny hives. My forehead was dotted with spots. My hair sat in useless half-curls about my ears. I lay in bed, unmoving. And then, when I looked as bad as could be, I found his number and called him.

"Hi, Sebastian. It's Ruby. I was wondering if you wanted to . . ."

"Hi, Ruby!" He was so bursting with good health and cheer that I had to plug my ears. "I'm going sailing this weekend. I'm running out the door right now."

"Sailing?"

"Yes, sailing. What do you think I do on weekends? Play basketball?"

"No. I never said that." I sank back into bed. "I'd better let you go."

"No, it's cool. Look, I've got to catch this train. But you can come with me."

"No, I don't think so."

"Come on! Meet me at Penn Station in half an hour."

"But I can't. I'm not ready."

"What are you wearing?"

"Just old shorts and a T-shirt."

"Then you're ready."

I met him at Penn Station, in half an hour, wearing what I had surmised to be a sailing outfit, strewn from the unhung heaps of clothes lying on the bedroom floor. I had on black ballet pumps, black pedal pushers that I had to struggle to zip, a white and navy horizontal-striped T-shirt that strained under the duress of Play-Doh breasts. I wore fresh red lipstick and large glasses tinted blue. The maybe-maybe hairdo was hidden under a yellow scarf tied around my head.

He met me, wearing flip-flops, paint-spattered surfer shorts, and a tank top that emphasized his broad shoulders and muscular arms. His hair was arranged in punky Afro twists, the one aspect of his appearance that appeared to have required effort and forethought.

He stretched his enormously long legs across the compartment, resting his feet on my thighs.

Though I darted my eyes away from him in what I had always taken to be the internationally acknowledged sign for "Stop talking now, please," Sebastian maintained a steady stream of conversation, most of it babble. Closing my eyes, I let the babble lick my limbs, like warm waves. He didn't seem to mind my zoning out. In fact, he too seemed to have zoned out, only through words rather than silence.

An hour passed amiably this way and I realized that one needn't understand someone, or even attempt to understand them, to find their presence soothing. We got off the train by the Jersey shore, where we were met by a middle-aged lady in a silver Range Rover.

"This is my mother." Sebastian's mother was about the same height as me but far more beautiful. She wore khakis, pink patent leather flats, and a white turtleneck. Around her swan neck hung a slim diamond crucifix that glittered in the sun. "Hello, Mrs. Chase. So nice to meet you." I wanted to add that I had heard so much about her, but I hadn't, except for in my own head.

They had an exhaustive library in their house. Check Chekhov, check Dostoevsky, check Sartre, check Henry James and Jane Austen, check stories of James Baldwin and plays of Harold Pinter. I couldn't find any embarrassing books, not one Jackie Collins or Len Deighton. On a top shelf I spied the autobiography of LL Cool J, but, reaching up to grab it, I found it stiff and unread, not a single page bent.

Mrs. Chase made spaghetti, while Sebastian wove his arms around his mother's trim waist. I beamed inwardly because mommy's boys are always good at cunnilingus. Mrs. Chase retired to her room to read and we got back into the car, trailing a cut-glass moon round the forks in the road.

Sebastian was determined that I should make acquaintance with his boat before we sailed it the next morning. I had been expecting a yacht, because of his mother's thinness and elegance, I suppose, and was shocked to find that he had been waxing lyrical over a tiny Sunfish. Charmed, I took his hand in mine.

"What is all that on your arms?" he asked, as we watched the moon to see if it was planning anything.

"Oh, those?" I answered coolly, as if I hadn't noticed them before. "I had an Iggy Pop moment."

"Just a moment?"

"Yes. Only a moment."

We slept in his childhood bed. He stripped to his boxers and loaned me a T-shirt. When he curled me under the crook of a huge arm, I began to cry.

"I love you," I whispered. I didn't, but I wanted to explain, to myself and to him, the parade of tears streaming down my cheeks, like floats in a carnival.

He pretended he hadn't heard me, as he wiped the tears away.

"Sorry this bed is so hard. Same bed I've had since I was fourteen."

I couldn't answer, and, nervous, he kept talking.

"I love sailing. My father taught me how to do it before he passed away. A white man's sport. I love skateboarding and snowboarding too. And surfing. I think skateboarding is hardest. With sailing, if you fall, it's on water. With snowboarding, if you fall, you fall on snow. But with skateboarding, when you fall, you're falling on concrete. I broke my ankle last summer on the Brooklyn Bridge. But that's still my favorite place to skateboard. I love it."

He kept saying the word love until, through my tears, I choked out a question. "Sebastian, who was the love of your life?"

He held me tighter as he recalled the love of his life, as though he were revealing an affair to a girlfriend he had been with for six years, restraining me against a crazed reaction. "Erica. She was a girl on the track team, back at college. We were together for five years, but then we kind of drifted apart. She's engaged now, to a banker. Why, who was the love of your life?"

"Liev," I sighed miserably.

"Who was he?" he demanded in the fake-soft tones of a man who was already jealous.

"Oh, he was just this vampire we had staying with us when I was twelve."

"Oh." Sebastian seemed satisfied with my response.

And then we went to sleep.

The next morning, he fixed eggs Florentine and coffee and picked me more appropriate footwear from his little sister's closet. Then we went down to the docks and he strapped a life jacket around my chest before placing me at the back of the boat.

"Weave!" "Duck!" "Tack!" "Mack!" I couldn't make out his instructions, as they spilled, rapid fire, from his plush lips.

"I DON'T UNDERSTAND WHAT YOU'RE SAYING," I sulked, and then, with greater force, "I don't understand what you're saying. I want to go back to New York." Under my breath I added, "You fake WASP motherfucker."

I hated the wind and the waves. I hated the sun and the sky. I hated the shoes he had made me wear. They were ugly. They were FUNCTIONAL.

"Calm down," he said. "Calm down."

For reasons I don't understand, I did calm down. I opened my eyes and the sun made me laugh. The waves and the wind and the sky made me happy. I liked his little sister's dorky deck shoes. Reflected in his perfect chest, my petulance bounced over the side of the boat and under the sea.

After a couple of hours, he tied the boat back onto the dock and we spilled into the shallow water: When we got home, we found a note from his mother saying that she had left for a garage sale. After showering off the sand, we crawled back into his schoolboy bed.

Sebastian smelled of brine and raucous good health. His skin was still warm from the sun. The hairs on his arms and the down on his chest were sunbaked to perfection, channeling the spirits of all the happy cats who had ever stretched on windowsills.

"I love you," I said again, although I didn't. I just wanted to think of an excuse to explain why I couldn't stop smiling. We took the train back to the city and when he went home, he took me with him. It was a week before, nervous as a burglar with bells glued to her shoes, I tiptoed back into my own apartment. Gathering a few outfits, moisturizer, deodorant, and my favorite underwear, I hopped a cab back to Sebastian's, where I already had my own toothbrush waiting by his sink.

Sebastian held my hand when we went out at night. He woke me up with kisses. He bought me presents with money he had earned from me. He only, once or twice, suggested it was perhaps time for me to go back to work, to call my agent back and hit some auditions. I was proud that I was with a beautiful black man. He was proud that he was with a semistar. The longer we spent together, the more the semi started to disintegrate, chopped first to demi, then quasi and finally pseudo. I was happy that way. He less so.

He didn't like working with actors or actresses he felt were less talented than me, less beautiful. He'd snap at the ones who flirted with him and they loved him even more: the personal assistant who cannot hide his contempt for his clients. He became all the rage. He got a job working for De Niro and he started earning good money, better than he had with me, which he used to blow on clothes. Shopping excited him. He dragged me around SoHo, to Helmut Lang, Prada, and Louis Vuitton. Seeing myself in the boutique mirrors, I looked like a grumpy child being taken to the Museum of Modern Art.

"I don't get it," I'd snarl, as he held up a three-quarter-length microfiber jacket for my delectation. "I want to go home."

Sebastian wanted to be my stylist.

"Sweetie, I thought you'd look so good in this color."

He'd sling an olive cashmere scarf around my neck and tie it and retie it until he was satisfied it was falling right. It was never falling right.

He bought me a Louis Vuitton traveling bag that had five zips.

"You think I'm going somewhere, Sebastian?"

"God, I hope not."

"Perhaps it's a good idea."

His eyes clouded and he took the bag back to the store and exchanged it for a bikini. He thought I was so much thinner than I was. I took it back and exchanged it for cash, which I put in his wallet that night as he slept. I don't know if he even noticed it. He never said anything. Most of the places he wanted to go, I couldn't have heard him anyway.

We went to parties with guest lists. We went to clubs with guest lists, velvet ropes, and VIP rooms within VIP rooms. He took happy drugs, up drugs that made him want to hug and kiss and squeeze me all the more. At every bar, at every club, in each and every VIP room, I made my child-bored-at-the-art-gallery face, until he said we could go home.

For a time, his skin maintained the immaculate glow of the chosen. Infuriated, I decided to suck it out for myself. "Why do you always want to give me blow jobs?" he queried one night, "Not that I'm complaining."

Not long after, I got carried away and he got frightened. "Ruby. RUBY! That's too rough. Honey, you're being too rough on me," and he pulled away to the other side of the bed.

"Why? Is it that girls aren't supposed to enjoy doing that? Is that the problem?" I screamed, slamming the bathroom door behind me.

"No, Ruby. No, I love it. I love you. Knowing that you like being with me is the best feeling in the world. But you were hurting me. I had to say something."

I looked in the bathroom mirror. Even with the draconian lighting I could see that my skin had acquired a rosy glow. Outside the door, Sebastian picked at a spot that was forming above his eyebrow.

It went downhill from there—his skin kept time with the disintegration of the relationship. I was gloriously robust, a punk-rock milk maiden. There was no longer a trace of fat, no wobble or flab. Just acres of creamy flesh and rosy cheeks. My agents finally had their call to Merchant Ivory returned.

I picked the spots on his back for him, squealing with delight as a blackhead wriggled, short and hard, from his anguished flesh. He no longer looked quite so fetching in his tank tops and handed them down to me, defeat in his eyes. My tiger-eye irises shining with glee, I slashed the tank tops into crop tops and wore them with pink bra straps hanging out.

At night, I felt greater compassion for Sebastian, felt guilty for all the darkness I had shown him. I saw it dancing in his dreadlocks and, as he slept, I tried to pick it out. It didn't work. Though I had put it there, I couldn't take it away. By then, he cried more than me and breathed choked dreams in and out of his short, straight nose all night long. I always slept under the crook of his arm, even though his arm was so thick and heavy, sometimes I could barely breathe. I would never move him or say so much as a word. I tried very hard to wake up in the exact same position in which I had fallen asleep.

Sebastian smoked his way through a particularly tense dinner. "Have you ever seen any plays by Chekhov?" I asked, picking at my risotto, then cut myself short. "No, of course you wouldn't have."

Sebastian stubbed his cigarette out. "Why do you do that to me? Why do you think I'm stupid? Unlike you, I actually went to college."

"To study English literature, so I hear."

"I have a good job," his voice rose.

"Sebastian, you're a whore. No, wait. You're not a whore."

"Thank you."

"No, you're a fucking pimp and that's worse."

He scrunched his face and turned away and when he turned back a tear slipped into his meal, a salty garnish on his spinach and mashed potato.

I always felt bad when he cried. He always felt bad when I cried. "I think we do this so that we can comfort one another," I whispered, taking his huge hand in my tiny one.

"I used to do that to my sister," he sniffled. "She was so independent, even when she was four years old. She would never let me hug her. So I would pinch her, scratch her, bite her good and proper until she was so upset, she'd let me hold her. She'd be in so much pain, she would temporarily forget that it was me who hurt her in the first place."

"I know," I soothed, kissing his cheek, "I know."

We paid the check and walked back to his apartment arm in arm. We lay on his bed, swathed in Irish linen, listening to Air and stroking each other's faces. He kissed me gently and smiled.

"I know how hard it is for you to be straight with me. And I want you to know, I believed you from the first moment you told me that you loved me. I know how much you care about me."

I kissed his forehead and, in tones of silk and sugar, sing-songed, "I don't love you. I don't love you and I don't care about you. I never did. I just had nothing to say to you and 'I love you' seemed as good a sentence as any."

Leaping out of bed, he backed himself against the bathroom door.

"What the fuck is wrong with you, Ruby? Why are you so fucking cruel?'

Following him out of bed, I leaned my head on his chest and laughed, "So much Louis Vuitton!"

"What? Speak in fuckin' English," he cried as he slammed me against the wall. "Speak in fuckin' English, you fucking bitch."

Sebastian sank to the floor, so tired of this, so ashamed that he had laid his hands on me, something he had never, ever done before.

I leaned against the wall, marks on both my arms where he had grabbed me, a smile tickling my mouth.

"So much baggage."

Seventeen

Costarring

Sean showed rushes of *Mean People Suck* to the backers. They hated it. They thought I was too unattractive. They thought he had indulged me too much. It was more graphic in its violence than they had expected. Most damning of all, they thought I had no chemistry with my costar. Was that Aslan's fault or mine? I had had over five years' experience as an actress. It was Aslan's first movie. He hadn't even wanted to act, but the casting director discovered him strumming a Gibson Sunburst in a guitar shop and persuaded him to audition.

The first time I ever met him he was leaving makeup, trundling down the steps of the trailer with headphones around his neck. He carried his Walkman in the deep pocket of his winter coat as if it were a gun: he needed it to walk the streets of Manhattan at one-thirty in the morning, even if it were just across the block to the set, his fingers ready to hit the play button at the first sign of danger. I had been filming all day and was going home to sleep. He was wearing tan cords, a beige duffel coat, and a loopy grin.

"Hello," I said.

"Good-bye," said Aslan.

His peers called him Aslan because they decided that he goes through his wardrobe at night into a whole other realm. Aslan was so mysterious that his hair and eyes and skin didn't have a specific color. Usually beauty is about definition—black hair, say, with bright blue eyes and alabaster skin. Aslan was a beauty and we didn't even know why, although we spent many evenings discussing him.

His shoulder-length hair was tousled and sort of dirty-brown, his skin was both tan and slightly jaundiced. His eyes might have been hazel if they weren't olive. Almost all of him was in earth tones, as if he had been created by a team of camouflage experts. When I asked the casting director, she claimed that he came from Colorado to play in a band and that when she found him in the guitar store, he was singing Steely Dan songs slightly off-key.

Aslan, we concluded, was that boy on the baseball field who stood off in a corner twirling as the game happened around him. He was the one humming to himself while the ball flew past his ear.

Sean had been adamant that we not meet each other until the last possible minute, since he feared it might adversely affect the authenticity of our relationship. The morning after I saw Aslan, I greeted Sean with the ultimatum that he introduce us NOW or I was planning on being very difficult. Sean dragged me by the arm and into the makeshift cafeteria where Aslan was having his breakfast.

"Aslan, this is Ruby," drawled Sean. I was wearing faded jeans and a worn T-shirt—both the jeans and T-shirt had been specially distressed by the costume designer who made them.

"I don't know you," he said happily, flashing a Chiclet-tooth smile that cut from ear to ear.

"That's okay, you don't need to know my films."

"No, I don't know you. I haven't met you before," and he bowed his head in formal introduction. Head still bowed, he peered at me with a luminous no-color eye through a strand of no-color hair arranged in no specific style.

"Yes you have!" I answered, my indignant shriek raising the director's hackles. "Yesterday, as you were leaving makeup."

He said he didn't remember. And, smiling, he moved away. Sean and I sat down at the table and Aslan returned with a banana, which he ate absentmindedly, entranced by a cobweb dangling from the chair. Every minute or so he would nod in agreement with some invisible power. Sean quickly excused himself to go to the bathroom. I cornered him outside the stall and screeched, "What the hell's up with that kid? He won't even talk to me."

"Lower your voice," whispered Sean. "Dude, Aslan has serious spirit guides in the form of prairie animals. He was probably just busy talking to them. Don't take offense. It's his first time on a movie set. What do you want from him?"

I just wanted to hold him. But I don't know what it was I wanted to hold, since it was only the second time I'd met him and there was nothing about him within my grasp: clouds in the shape of Ireland, premonitions about the deaths of celebrities, the bass line from a

Rolling Stones B-side. Aslan existed in too many forms for the room. At least Sebastian Chase, who did not exist at all, had created a body of taut, contoured muscle for me to cling to. If I could just fuck Aslan, if I could feel him inside me, I might know why I was so touched by him. I might know that he had some semblance of a notion that he was touching me too. And that maybe, just maybe, I was touching him.

Weaving back from the bathroom, my cheeks flushed pink with determination, I sat beside him at the table. By now, we were the only ones in the cafeteria. Sean, sensing that keeping us apart for so long had maybe not been so smart after all, had strategically closed it off and shut the doors, so that we could get to know each other. I had no idea if he could act, but Aslan's energy was so intense; it prickled and boiled, ruffling my hair and confidence. I waited and waited for him to acknowledge me, sitting so close to him that, if I hadn't just lost five pounds, our thighs would be touching. But he stared stoically ahead.

"Do you hate me?"

He shook his head and smiled.

"Do you like me?"

He nodded.

Then we both stared straight ahead. Finally, I turned to him and heard myself ask, "Please, will you touch my hand." He turned to face me for the first time, as if I had said something so shocking he had to make sure I was for real. Very slowly, as if licking a potentially dangerous berry, he traced a finger across my palm. Satisfied that it was not going to kill him, he placed his hand full on mine;

no fingers intertwined, it just hovered, like a Japanese train, never touching the tracks, riding on electrical energy.

His hand gave off such heat, my knees started to shake. His hand didn't move and he resumed his cobweb trance. The heat traveled up my arm, down my stomach and, as the sound of Sean yelling at a prop boy wafted into the hall, I felt myself come. I didn't know if Aslan could tell what had happened. After it was done he stood up and walked away. I waited for him. I waited and ten minutes later I went to see what had happened. Aslan had left the building and would not return to the set until they dragged him out of the guitar store from whence they had first plucked him.

"Ruby," pleaded Sean, as we waited for him to return so that we could shoot our first scene together, "try and be nice. You may even learn something from him. You might have spent time on the West Coast, but Aslan has spent time on a different plain."

By lunchtime I was kissing him. Again and again, with a gun in my hand. They had to keep cutting and starting again because Aslan couldn't be persuaded to kiss with his mouth open. Eventually they decided to position my head so that the audience couldn't see what a cold kisser Aslan was, our kiss implied but never seen, as though we were Hays Code lovers.

That bad kiss sealed it for me: I was infatuated with him and I hadn't even got through the first day yet. I was consumed with the need to know how he really kissed, so certain was I that he was faking. When I put this to Sean he didn't even bother pulling his coffee cup from his lips.

"Well of course he's *faking*. This isn't real."

And yet with each day that passed—admittedly our romance was shot out of sequence—I got further and further away from ever getting to kiss him "for real." He would arrive on the set, do his scenes, and then leave without saying good-bye. If he had not said good-bye *only* to me, I would have taken it as a sign. But he didn't say good-bye to anyone, so I couldn't pretend to feel singled out.

We didn't have any scenes together for a couple of days and I felt disconsolate. I had gotten used to his silences—they were never sullen—and his constant smile. Finally I called him late one night. "Hey, you," he said as if it was the third time we had spoken that day. He was easy-going and giggly, unconnected to the space elf that I had starred with over the last few weeks.

"Uh, do you want to come over and listen to music?"

"Yes," he pondered briefly, "I do."

The doorbell rang a few minutes later, before I had the chance to put on mascara. I rationalized that it couldn't be him, Aslan lived way downtown. It must be a messenger from Sean, new pages he wanted me to look at. I buzzed the door and there he was, no-color hair over no-color eyes in less defined a fashion than ever before.

He shrugged off his coat and flopped onto the bed like a man who had just come back from the steelworks. In fact, he had spent the day laying down tracks in the studio. He boasted that he had written two of them all by himself. I asked him what the first song was called. Aslan blinked his eyes. He clearly had not thought about this yet. " 'Pendulum.' " And the second song? " 'Pensioner,' " he replied proudly, the corners of his mouth curling up.

His mouth was always curling, whether it was up or down, like a novelty fish you put in your palm, a sliver of red fortune. Except they don't tell your future. They tell your mood, for people who aren't sure what they're feeling. The red fish says "Passionate," "Sad," "Angry," with the tiniest flick of its tail or curl on its side. Either this means that it takes very little effort to be passionate, sad, or angry. Or that it's easy to slip into the place where you wouldn't know what you were feeling if it weren't for a novelty fish. That's why you get them in crackers. It's like a safety kit: no one ever knows what they're feeling at the holidays. All they really feel is the turkey inside them, pressing hard against their gullet like a lie.

Aslan's mouth curled up and stayed there. He was in such a good mood, so pleased with himself, so pleased with me. I tried to think of something to say to this boy who, for all he had revealed, might as well be mentally subnormal, and I couldn't think of anything. I could feel everything, but I couldn't speak it. The everything lodged itself in my throat like a student sit-in, stubborn and pointless. While he went to the bathroom, I flipped through my diary to remind myself I knew how to use words. I fell upon a page in bold lettering, and when he came back, I said it out loud: "You are my connect-the-dots boy."

I knew what I meant. That I had from him but the slimmest of clues with which to form a man. That he was my creation. That he was incomplete without me to fill him in. That having taken the time and effort to invent him, connect-the-dots boy had me so hard, it didn't matter that he was constructed from paper and pencil rather than flesh and blood.

I didn't tell him how many connect-the-dots men there have been over the years. I didn't have to tell him that he had given me even less to go on than ever before. He lay on the bed and I sat in the chair by my desk. Then he sat in the rocking chair and I lay on the bed. I stretched my arms above my head, to expose white belly, flat and unscarred, a flash of clean light in a body imperfect.

He lay next to me, baby-blue hooded sweatshirt worn inside out. Then I got up and cracked open a beer. It should have been red wine, but I just wanted to pace and pretend, unscrew things, because he was making me so hot. I was starting to melt, and by the time he kissed me, I was out of my body. I looked down on us as he put his hand in my hair (dot), stroked my back (dot), took my shirt off (dot), unhooked my bra (dot), took his sweatshirt off (dot). Connect the dots, connect the dots. Play by yourself like a good girl.

I was shocked at his finely tuned body—even better than Sebastian's. It meant something. A boy like Aslan didn't need a body like that. It means something, broad shoulders and stomach muscles on a boy with unwashed hair. The muscles seemed like something he was looking after as a favor to a friend. They meant, I said out loud, that once he had been with a girl who needed him so much he had had to build a body so that she would have something to cling to. "No, I built a wall. I was trying to keep her out."

"Did it work?"

"I moved to New York, didn't I?"

"And she's still in Colorado?"

"I don't know."

He cared, which is why he had not tried to find out. He cared about a girl and I scuttled back into my body like a child chastised.

Suddenly I could feel his tongue, hot and wet, his Chiclet teeth, cold as tombstones. He put his fingers inside me. That was the end. He let me moan, once, twice, catch my breath as I rode his fingers. And then he stopped, turned away, put his shirt back on. I tried to kiss him, embarrassed bemused kiss. He patted my face, looking away. Then he smiled slash passion fish smile, picked up my bra from the floor and draped it over my arms. Eyes burning with shame, I scooped my breasts into the cups and he carefully hooked the back, grinning at his own deftness. Then he was asleep beside me and I was awake, staring out the window, New York Street Scene No. 2.

What did I do wrong? What did I do wrong, dog dragging paja-ma'd owner to mailbox? What did I do wrong, trash overflowing? What did I do wrong, screenless television dumped on sidewalk? What did I do wrong, van delivering tomorrow's newspapers? Dog turns his head to answer. Tomorrow's newspaper bears the same news:

"He knows you're crazy. He knows you're sick. He felt it inside you. It's written in Braille, raised white flesh on the inside of your vagina. Everything you've done wrong, everyone you've upset, your mother, Liev, Sebastian Chase. That's why he ran away. Because you feel disgusting. Because he couldn't pretend you are just a beautiful girl. He doesn't care. The prairie animals warned him about a girl like you. They said there would be signs. He liked your eyes, your mouth, so he wanted to touch you, to smell you and lick your pret-tiness. But as soon as he got inside he knew you were the one they had warned him about. And he will never, ever touch you again."

And he never did touch me again or allow me to touch him. He woke up to find me still gazing out the window. Usually I would pretend to be asleep. This time I did not, eyes Winona wide, gamine gameplan: help me, I am small with big eyes, baby small, baby cute. Babies are designed not to have their heads bashed in and people who do that go to jail forever. He knew my eyes were open, but he pretended I was asleep instead, and crept around the apartment gathering his belongings. I waited for him to slip me a morning kiss hello. But he scooped the kisses from the floor with his clothes and stuffed them in the pocket of his jeans to save for a girl who wasn't crazy.

I scurried to the door as I heard it open, in pink bra and panties. I tried to kiss him but he turned his head. His earphones were already around his neck and his hand was in his pocket with the Walkman. "Good-bye," said Aslan, smiling, and hit play.

I peered out the window, waiting, at least, to watch him disappear up Bleecker Street. But he never disappeared because he never reappeared, although I heard the front door slam. Frustrated at not even being able to admire him as he walked away, I went back to bed, crossing and uncrossing my legs, trying to get comfortable, pulling the whole duvet over my head, then pulling it back and kicking my legs around it. My eyelashes scratched me. My knees touching made me feel sicker than ever. I had a toothache. But there was something else. Something softer but more troublesome than the hair falling on my forehead. It was his fingerprints, deep inside me. I kicked and squirmed some more. But they would not fade.

I saw him every day for the next week. But he never saw me again.

He said hello, eyes on cobweb, at floor, on hands clenched tight at his sides. He wasn't unpleasant. But he was afraid, protective. He was a good person and he struggled valiantly not to be one of those boys who screws a girl and then ignores her. He didn't ignore the girl because he didn't screw the girl because he didn't try. He would be thrown out of L.A. forever and ever. At the end of the week he was done on the film, but I had to stay an extra three days. For some reason I expected him to ring at the end of them and ask how it had gone or, at the very least, turn up at our small and poorly catered wrap party. But he didn't.

"You'll see him soon enough," soothed Sean when I confided how much I liked him. "After all, you'll be doing all the film festivals together."

"Fat chance," I thought, convinced, with each day that had passed, post-kiss, that CAA had been right to ignore *Mean People Suck*.

"Why don't you just call him?" asked Sean, and thus encouraged, I made him stand beside me when I finally did.

"Hey, Aslan. It's Ruby. What's up?" Breezy, light, happy fun girl, kiss me, no darkness in me.

"I'm watching the television."

"Oh. What's on?" GIGGLE. NO DARKNESS IN ME. Fucking help me out here.

"Nothing. I'm just watching the television." Silence.

"Do you want some company? Can I come over and watch the television with you?"

"Um . . . no."

He didn't answer quick enough for me to think there was a girl there. His response wasn't the quick-draw response that precurses a lie. He answered slow because he was prepared to tell the truth.

"So, Aslan," laugh small, darkness in me big, seeping from my cunt into the receiver, down the telephone line, "do you just want to be left alone?"

"Yes," his words curled up at either end, "I do."

I left Sean standing there, and went home, where I crawled into bed, crushed. Appalled at his honesty. When I woke up at six-thirty A.M., drowning in the waves of shame washing across the sheets, I determined that I would not be going back to sleep and headed out for a bagel. Still in my pajamas, I pulled a fleecy coat across my shoulders and stumbled up Bleecker to the 24-hour diner. The diner was packed with flush-faced gay boys winding down after a night's clubbing. I took a corner booth across from two men with matching peroxide buzz cuts and black lycra T-shirts. They glanced at me, disheveled and spilling jelly on my wrist, and shot each other excited "minor celebrity gossip" looks.

When I got home an hour later, to my utter disbelief, the empty vessel had left a message on my answering machine.

"Hey, Ruby. It's Aslan. Calling you. On the telephone. Alexander Graham Bell. Belle and Sebastian. Sebastian was your lover, right? I'm sure he loved you very much. Anyway, when you get this message . . . you should ring me back. Okay? Okay. Peace."

And there was peace.

Eighteen

The New World Order

I shrugged off my coat, ran myself a bath. I shampooed my hair and shaved my legs, although I had shaved them the preceding evening, just before I rang him, sure he would come over and we would make love. This time I was certain. He rang me. Very early in the morning. When men don't ring you it's because they don't want to. When they ring you it's because they want you. And when they ring very late or very early it's because they are tortured by erotic thoughts of you and simply cannot wait for a more suitable hour to call.

I pulled on jeans and a sweater, mascara and lip gloss morning makeup, and carried my cell phone in my purse. "Hi. I've been out jogging. I just checked my messages. Should I come by? I'm right near your house. You live on Avenue A, don't you?"

"You've jogged all this way?"

"Yeah, I jog every morning."

"Good."

I pinched my cheeks flushed and shooed the cab away. Aslan answered the door with his headphones around his neck, the wire coiling across his baby-blue sweatshirt like a licorice rope. His sleeves were hanging past his hands. He yanked them up to his bony elbows, the only element of skinny indie rock boy on his finely cut body.

"Can I have some water."

I leaned to use the tap.

"Don't do that. It's bad. It's stolen water and then they pump it back to us all fucked up, all full of chemicals and bad vibes."

He reached into the small fridge and retrieved an enormous container of mineral water. I pulled the hood of his blue sweatshirt flirtatiously over his brow and he pulled away from me, flirtatiously, I felt. I felt the flirtation rising real in his jeans and he felt his way out of the kitchen and onto his bed. I followed, placing myself, literally, at his feet.

"Ruby, I rang you on the phone, early this morning, because . . . early this morning I was thinking about something I needed to make clear. I just wanted to explain something. So now you're here, in my house and now I can . . . in my house."

"Okay." He let me kiss him.

"Okay, Ruby. I need to explain to you that we can't be together and why it is, in fact, that I can have no sexual or romantic relations with you at all."

"Okay," I nodded, leaning in to kiss him and again he let me.

"Ruby, I'm not looking for a lover right now."

"Okay," I nodded, touching my mouth to his in agreement.

"Ruby. At the end of any relationship there is a check to pay. And with you it would be a very big check. A check that I cannot afford."

I took my tongue out of his mouth and murmured, "I'll pay it, silly billy. I've got money."

"I don't like money . . ."

"So let me handle it."

"Oh God, don't talk about handling money. Handling money, the physical day-to-day process of touching dollar bills with the flesh on our fingers, is what's making us ill."

I put my tongue back in my own mouth and blinked my eyes in bemusement.

"Why do you think Donald Trump is so ugly? Or Rupert Murdoch? Have you ever stopped to wonder why, why do millionaires, billionaires, tycoons, and thieves look the way they do? Did Donald Trump always look like that? Did Andrew Lloyd Webber always look like that? No, they were ordinary little boys and ordinary men, and then they happened to rub their bodies in bills and it infected their blood. They're only half alive. You're still beautiful, Ruby, but you're only half alive."

"Jesus Christ! I'm not that rich!" and I pulled as far away from him as the room would allow because, although he had said I was beautiful, he had also used the word "ugly" in a nearby sentence.

"You were in that movie last summer, right? You'll be in another movie this summer. You're rich enough."

"So you're not going to get involved with me because I make too much money?"

"Yes."

"Fine," I spat and stormed out in a huff which is, at least, cheaper than a taxi. I huffed all the way back to my apartment, where I stopped huffing and cried instead. "I want Sebastian, I want Sebastian to be here," I wailed to myself.

Aslan had made a moral choice and it was final. It didn't matter what I wore or if I washed my hair and shaved my legs in voodoo anticipation of ensnaring him. He would not bite. The only route left to me was that of understanding and modesty. I practiced my expressions long and hard in my bathroom mirror.

"Aslan," I breathed, cornering him "by accident" at his local bodega, "I know you've made a decision about me, and I respect it. I understand it. I mean, I don't understand it. Not at all. But I understand that it has been made with what you deem good reason, and I would not disrespect you by asking you to bend your rules for me, who is nothing, who is no more than a silly little film actress."

He felt bad and started defending me against my own harsh judgment. He was more friendly for a while. He tolerated me. He went record shopping with me, smiling slyly when the manager asked for my autograph. We ended up with a fifty percent discount, and Aslan, for all his money fears, could not have been more thrilled. Piling record on top of record, he selected a beginner's introduction to the music of John Coltrane and Thelonious Monk. No words. Notes all over the place. I tried desperately to find the rhythm because I thought that if I could I would be able to find him.

We were walking down Rivington when two men doing research for Ford cars asked us if they could pay us ten dollars to ask us some questions. The researcher was a nervous young man. He took a breath as though trying not to mess up his big break, and then asked, "What do you think of when I say 'Chevy'?"

I tilted my head and smiled reassuringly, wondering if the young man was bugged out because it was me, or because of Aslan's eyes.

"Chevy? I'd say 'All American'."

The young man cleared his throat again.

"And what do you think of when I say 'BMW'?"

Aslan blinked his see-through eyes at the blue sky. "Bob Marley and the Wailers."

The young man gave us the money. Aslan, of course, would not touch it.

"You hold it for me." And I had such hope in my heart that he asked me to hold it so that I could owe him something which meant we would see each other again, which was almost the same thing as being in a relationship.

He so did not want to have a relationship with me. He glowed with the aura of "Just doing my duty by a troubled youth," although he was a month younger than me. Anytime I tried to touch him, even brushing his elbow to make a point, he pulled away. He pulled far, far away like the seats at a Rolling Stones show that are so far back, the curve of the earth obscures your view of Keith Richards. At first he answered my questions in half-sentences, half-hearted, half-heard. After a week of me dropping by unannounced, he would answer the door with his hand in front of his face. Talk to the hand 'cause the ears won't listen. It could have been a Jerry Springer gesture. But it wasn't Jerry, it was Jedi.

Emma Forrest

The second to last time I saw him, we went to buy a sandwich at a shabby café near Chinatown. We were sitting at the counter as all around us dope deals went down in between bites from tofu rolls. Veganism and drug addiction. That sums up the neighborhood. The guy serving us was preternaturally angry, with tattoos all up his arms, which made me laugh. You can't look that nasty and then actually act that mean too. The guy with the arm tattoos is supposed to be a pussycat. But not this one.

Aslan ordered vegetarian sandwich number two before changing his order, after conferring briefly with a pot of swizzle sticks, to vegetarian sandwich number one. "Well which is it?" barked the man and all eleven of his arm tattoos stared daggers at us.

"Vegetarian sandwich number one. Um, no, number three."

"Oh for Christ's sake," spat the man.

Aslan looked up from the swizzle sticks, his eyes turning gray, the pupils approximating something like anger. "Forget about the sandwich," he hissed. Rising from his stool at the counter, he began to hook his backpack over his broad shoulders.

The guy got all hard-style, bellowing, "You're still going to have to pay for the sandwich, you little fuck—I've already started chopping the tomato." Without a word, Aslan took money from his back pocket, slammed it on the counter and began to back out of the café, never taking his newly gray eyes from the waiter. The guy and his eleven tattoos looked suddenly confused and I even felt sorry for him when he meekly asked, "So do you want the sandwich to go?" Aslan just held his hand in front of his face and walked out. I followed him and asked what was up. "I don't give a damn about

99

the money," his voice was trembling; "money is dirty. There's too much bad energy coming from that guy for me to eat a sandwich touched by his hands. I couldn't allow that kind of energy to enter my body." And he stormed off up the street. I went back in and rescued what had become vegetarian sandwich number one. Handing it to a homeless man who didn't seem too interested in my random act of kindness, I rushed to catch up with Aslan.

Charging down Avenue B, he picked a café he had found to be acceptable, and sat down at a table. He carefully peeled the remaining three dollars from his pocket and laid them down on the table so he could give me a detailed explanation of the problems with a one-dollar bill. Flipping a bill over with his knife, he gestured to the pyramid on the back. "See that pyramid? I mean, what the fuck is that doing there? I'll tell you: it's a masonic symbol. And see the writing beneath it, in Latin? Do you know what that means in English? Well, I'll tell you: it means 'New World Order.'"

He was interrupted midflow by the waiter bringing us water. Aslan gulped it down in one go. Wiping his mouth on his baby-blue sleeve, he turned to me and, leaning close enough to kiss, whispered, "Drink lots of water."

"Okay." I didn't ask why, but he felt it his duty to tell me.

"The head of the New World Order lives in a building in Connecticut. That building has the highest water bill in all of America. No one knows why. I know why."

He waited for me to ask, taking pleasure in my presence for the first time since the night he had fondled my breasts.

"Why does it have the highest water bill in America, Aslan?"

His mouth turned up at the corners, his lips erect with delight.

"Because the New World Order is stealing all the water. Humans are made up of seventy percent water. The earth is made up of seventy percent water. They're stealing it. So, please, Ruby . . . drink as much water as you can."

"Okay. Um, can I kiss you now?"

"No, baby, no you can't." And he leaned his forehead on mine. Then he got up and left, the miso soup he had ordered ending its life as Aslan's second uneaten snack of the day, as inconsequential as Rupert Everett's second lover in a Merchant Ivory film. A thought struck him as he closed the door of the café, and Aslan popped his head back inside.

"Ruby?"

"Yes, Aslan? Yes?"

"Remember to drink lots of water."

Nineteen

Maybe he just doesn't fancy her

Ruby? What can I say? I mean. Wow. What can I say? She's got the power. She's got the power. She's got the ruby slippers, right there on her beautiful Ruby feet. And she doesn't even know it. I can't mess with her, you know? I ain't gonna mess with her.

Part Two

Twenty

A challenge

Ruby's cards came postmarked New York, although they might as well have been postmarked Hades. By that time, I had built Ruby into a Roman goddess of desire, risen up from the underworld to take my husband away. I imagined her carved from white marble, standing in a museum, schoolchildren giggling at her naked white breasts.

I was going through Scott's briefcase, looking for this month's *Vanity Fair,* when I found the first card. It was a picture of the Statue of Liberty. At first, I was so crazed that I thought Ruby had written on the back of a photo of herself. And then I remembered New York and Staten Island, something about a ship full of immigrants and a lady with a lamp welcoming them. The cold. The hungry. The disillusioned by ten years of marriage.

"Hope all is well on the West Coast. I will see you in a few months." I pictured her living in the torch, peering, cold, across the water, marble in oxidized copper. "Of course," I reasoned, "statues don't stand in line for stamps," and I adapted the story in her head, so that the white marble was in fact an elaborate Alexander McQueen dress. Knowing what I did about her, it would not be too far-fetched to imagine Ruby wearing Alexander McQueen to run her errands.

I saw her once in real life, at a black-tie charity gala. Ruby was wearing jeans, moccasins, and a ripped Sex Pistols tank top. Scott had commented on how dirty she looked. The next day she was photographed shopping for groceries in a $5,000 backless Halston gown.

The beautician, dutifully, ran the current through the sparse, pale hairs on my upper lip. I jolted and shivered and thought about how much I hated my life. Every time my skin was steamed and squeezed, I prayed that the beautician would leap back, alarmed by the hideous black sludge emerging from my pores. But nothing came out. It wasn't a completely wasted session. It hurt just enough to make my eyes tear and heart harden.

I didn't care a damn about Scott, not anymore. I cared about what he was doing, and who he was doing it with, why and what I had done wrong, but not about him. He was irrelevant now.

I found it when I got home, in the sleeve of an Elvis Costello record. Scott kept his vinyl proudly, as if to say, "I may be a fuck-off powerful Hollywood producer but I can still get down." He had the CDs too. He had them both, just in case. In case he met a vengeful God. As if buying more, rather than less, would save him.

It was a postcard of the Brooklyn Bridge.

"It is so beautiful, I thought this was a good reason to write. This is just a quick note to say 'hi!,' lighter than the last time I wrote. I miss you. I will see you soon. Love Ruby xoxo."

"But 'xoxo' does not mean anything," I fumed, hating Ruby more than ever before. "It's so arbitrary: some random letters from a typewriter because there is no way to express what we really feel. It is an attempt to abbreviate emotion, to make it small and unthreatening. The x is a stamp of desire and the o, what is that anyway? A hug? A never-ending circle of insecurity and need?"

I suddenly felt sorry for her, grasping at a reason to write to him. I needed to know why this was so much lighter than the last time she wrote. I thought about her all the time. When Scott and I made love, not only was he imagining I was Ruby, but so was I, trying to remember what it was to be wanted.

This invisible girl-child, ripped Versace ghost-woman, had come to represent the focus of my life, of my work. My mother was dead. My father was long dead. I had no career. My marriage was in tatters. Ruby was all I had to live for.

Twenty-one

A ghost

I saw Ruby in the uptown Prada, the night before Christmas, but at first I didn't believe it was her. I hid in the dressing room and peered out from between the curtains. Surely Ruby was thinner than that? Taller? Didn't Ruby have famously beautiful skin and hazel eyes? This girl was sawn off at the knee, her eyes were dead and her skin was blotchy. Would I rather that *was* Ruby and she was uglier than I had thought, or that it was too ugly to be Ruby and wasn't her at all? I had wanted to come face to face with her for so long, but not if she wasn't beautiful. Not if she couldn't give me something to stew over, an excuse to dawdle, daydream, and procrastinate. Now how was I going to waste the next six months?

I turned back to the mirror, willing her to vanish before I did something stupid. And just as I was zipping myself into a pencil skirt, trying not to concentrate on loftier things, like rowing machines and reading groups, the curtains were pulled apart and there she was. It was definitely her: blotchy, stocky, and luminous. Nothing was in place. Not her hair, not her body, not her ill-fitting clothes. Her parka was soaked and she was trailing snow all through the store. I grabbed at a shirt to cover my breasts.

"I'm sorry," slurred Ruby, "I didn't know anyone was in here."

I stared at her transfixed, until Ruby giggled, "Do I know you?"

Still holding the blouse against my breasts, which I assessed, in a glance, to be smaller and firmer than Ruby's, I whispered, "I'm Scott's wife."

Ruby was unruffled. "Oh yeah. Scott from L.A. How is he?"

"We're getting divorced." It sounded rather merry when I said it out loud. "What are you doing here?" And that sounded ruder than asking how the husband who was divorcing me was. Something about Ruby makes every response an attack. All Ruby's questions, on the other hand, no matter how nosy or insensitive, are always retreats, unquestions that demanded nothing more than silence.

"I'm buying my Christmas presents," offered Ruby, more than happy to chat, even if it was to the woman whose marriage she had destroyed months earlier.

"Who are you buying for? My husband?" I asked, turning away to put on my bra. Before I could stop her, Ruby had leaned forward and hooked the ends of the brassiere together for me.

I shivered as her fingers touched my back. She admired her work, then snapped out of her reverie as I asked her again. She answered, dreamy, as though she and I were lying side by side at a slumber party.

"Who am I buying for? Myself. You probably read about it in Page Six."

"No," I said, pulling my turtleneck over my head, "I don't read the tabloids."

"Oh. Well, I'm the teenage starlet spending Christmas alone because my mother killed herself, tragically, some years ago, and I don't get along with my dad. My agent let me go just recently. I loved someone once but he went away. I had someone who loved me, but I asked him to leave. It's so stupid. I haven't been a teenager for two years now. And I'm fucking Jewish, for Christ's sake."

"Jewish, for Christ's sake?"

"Yes. I don't celebrate Christmas."

"I see."

Her pupils dilated as she brought me back into focus. "Scott and I aren't together anymore. We were never together. Can you see us together?"

"Can you see us together?"

"No."

Ruby waited for me while I lined up my purchases at the cash register. I wanted to shoo her away like the bedraggled sex kitten she was: "Go away, you silly little slut!" But I didn't.

She trailed me out the door, a grubby hand at my elbow, like a child. Outside, a photographer began to snap at Ruby. And then, to my horror, I realized he was photographing both of us together.

Twenty-two

The hustle

Ruby grabbed Rachel by the arm and hustled her into a cab. Shocked, Rachel turned to her traveling companion and asked, "Do you know where you're going to?"

"Do you like the things that life is showing you?" grinned Ruby, believing herself to be infallibly endearing. Her gums were bleeding.

Rachel gritted her teeth and asked again: "Where are you going?"

"I don't know," Ruby shrugged her sloping little shoulders. "With you, I guess."

She didn't ask Rachel if she wanted her to, or if that were okay. It was the night before Christmas and she had nowhere else. Rachel was supposed to be going to dinner at the home of another secular Jew. Like her, she was a woman who celebrated by buying gifts and drinking champagne and fighting and having make up sex. There would be no make up sex for Rachel this time around and, more regrettably, not even any fighting, which she secretly believed was what kept her invigorated and slim.

Ruby was much smaller than she had any right to be, soft and curvy with no hint of muscle at all beneath her milky white skin.

Rachel, in contrast, was tall, slender, with long legs and taut arms. The extreme New York cold made her hair shinier than ever. Ruby's hair was starting to grow in from the nail scissor disguise she had given herself when she walked out on Scott, and it fell in waves around her eyebrows, which were plucked in silent-film-star semi-circles. They were the only manicured part of her body, and these she had had attended to only because there had been a friendly makeup artist at the photo shoot three days before.

The magazine stylist was not so kind. She had been unable to hide her disgust at Ruby's inability to fit into a size four. Angrily tearing at the racks of beautiful clothes, she picked out a gold lamé sheath that fit, but made Ruby look like a Las Vegas hooker. As soon as the editor saw the contacts, the pictures were killed.

Rachel pulled her turtleneck past her chin as she took in the extent of Ruby's blotches and bloating. She couldn't imagine Scott wanting her. She couldn't imagine him having any patience with her. And then, the more she thought about it, the more she realized that she couldn't imagine him, period. Not what he looked like, or smelled like, or how his voice sounded. He was gone from her memory bank after barely three months apart. And she didn't feel sad about it. Not about that. But she did feel sad, unutterably so, because she knew what wasn't making her unhappy. "Knowing what doesn't make you unhappy," she sulked, "is more painful than knowing what does make you unhappy. It leaves you with greater responsibility toward your own state of mind." She could tell that Ruby fell into the former category.

Ruby shifted from shoe to shoe outside Rachel's apartment. "So, Scott's ex, can I come up?"

Rachel, liking the sound of "Scott's ex," decided she could.

Twenty-three

Appraisal

They looked at each other for a while.

Ruby looked at the photos on Rachel's dressing table. She looked at her computer that hadn't been switched on. The maple-wood desk held rows of framed photos of babies gurgling, an elderly couple on a sofa, a hard-bodied man playing with a wrinkly puppy in front of a fire.

"Is this your family?" asked Ruby.

Rachel steered her away from the desk. "No."

"Oh. Well, who are they?"

"Those are just prints from photo sessions I did."

"You're a photographer?'

"Yes."

"And these are the pictures you're proudest of?"

"Yes."

"Well then, why aren't they on your walls, blown up big? Why are they on your desk, by your computer, in these funny little ornate frames?"

"They're not funny. They're solid silver."

"Whatever. Why are they so small? When you make something stay small, that means you really care about it. You want to be able to carry it with you if you have to flee on foot. Why do you care about a model you posed in front of a fire or some old people you don't even know?"

Rachel didn't answer. Ruby walked around the room, touching things. She absentmindedly ran her stubby fingers through a bowl of chocolate nonpareils, as though mistaking them for the hair of a lover. She opened a cigarette case and took a pink Sobranie to play with. She held it grandly between two fingers as she leafed through magazines and plucked books from the shelves. Rachel felt it more sharply when Ruby touched her photos and her books than when she had touched her back. Hands clenched in discomfort, she walked into the kitchen to put the kettle on. When she came back, Ruby was trying on her new Gucci trenchcoat. She looked like a child prostitute hidden in the folds of a pervert's raincoat.

She took it off and, though she tried to hang it back up, it was all wrong and Rachel had to tell her. Rachel eyed her hacked hair; her body that went in and out in all the wrong places; her chewed lips and nails. "You. You are all wrong."

"I know!" Ruby squealed with delight at the recognition. Over-excited, she sank into the sofa, a dark look bleeding across her face.

Rachel turned the hanger so that the coat was facing the same way as all her others, a rod of down-filled Gucci. "What do you eat?"

Ruby had a fistful of chocolates in her red mouth. "Nothing," she said, a nonpareil slipping down her chin.

"You don't look like you eat nothing." Rachel paused long enough to decide she needn't say the next sentence, then said it anyway. "I don't think you should be eating quite so many of those." Her tone was that of an underpaid, over-age babysitter.

She felt ashamed as Ruby held back tears. Still, she thought, "Please don't let her cry." She didn't want to have to comfort her.

"My agent says I shouldn't eat like that either. My former agent." Ruby clasped a throw cushion to her tummy. "I eat mainly at the cake shop across the street from my apartment. The women who work there are very thin. Like you. There's a thin Asian girl. A thin black girl. A thin blond. It looks like Scott's casting office," she added, giggling.

She didn't apologize because she was too far gone to know she had said anything wrong. Rachel felt a wave of unease as she realized that they were discussing her husband, whom Ruby had stolen away because she was bored.

"You should date rock stars. There was this one who wanted to throw me out of a window. I didn't mind. I thought it would be a pretty great way to die. He chickened out though."

Sick of her babble, Rachel interrupted, "So what was the sex with Scott like?"

"I don't know," huffed Ruby, suddenly demure.

"You fucked my husband. You must know what he was like."

"I never know about . . . stuff like that. Intercourse."

Rachel looked at the red-faced little girl and felt like a sixty-year-old biology teacher forced to cover the facts of life. But no one was forcing her. And yet she could not stop.

"What did he like?"

"I don't know."

"Did he ask you to put a finger up his ass?"

"No!" she screamed and hid her face behind the throw cushion.

Rachel pried the pillow away. "He liked me to do that."

Ruby was sobbing, her small shoulders moving up and down like an unsafe merry-go-round.

"Please. I don't want to talk about it anymore. I want to go home." She picked up her bag and scurried to the door.

"No," said Rachel. "It's snowing too hard. Stay here. Stay in the spare room." Ruby looked at her nervously. Rachel smiled, as naturally, as genuinely as she could.

"I'll cook you dinner."

"No! You're just inviting me to the prom so that you can pour a bucket of pigs' blood on my head."

"No. I'm not. It's nasty outside. We're both hungry. I love cooking. I'll make you salmon pasta."

"Really?" She let her bag sink to the floor and followed it seconds later. Leaning against the wall, Ruby whispered, "I can't remember the last time I had a meal that someone actually cooked."

"You've been to restaurants, right?" laughed Rachel, trying to get her to snap out of it.

Ruby stayed serious. "I mean, someone who wasn't obscured

from view by swinging metal doors. If I can't see them cook it, then it doesn't count."

Rachel looked at the food while she cooked, glancing up now and then at Ruby, perched awkwardly on a stool at the kitchen counter.

"I dreamed about you," Rachel announced, bringing the pasta to a boil. "The last few weeks I was with Scott, he was dreaming about you so much that I started dreaming about you too."

Ruby, coming back to life, couldn't begin to fathom an appropriate response. "I guess you get that kind of closeness when you've been with someone as long as you two had."

"Yes, you do. But he was in love with you."

"How unfortunate for him," snorted Ruby.

"It was unfortunate for him. And for me."

Ruby stared at her shoes. "I'm sorry."

"It's not your fault. I don't think it's your fault. Do you like your pasta al dente?"

"Yes."

As she ate her meal she started to cry.

"Why are you crying?" asked Rachel. She did not sound kind. She did not sound unkind. She sounded disinterested.

"Because I am sad." She wiped away a rivulet of tears. "You don't understand how hard my job is."

"Ha!" spat Rachel. "Acting's not hard!"

"No, not acting. That's what I do to make money, but it isn't my job. My real job is to make men realize that the hot young girl isn't worth it. That the hot young girl is nowhere near as good in bed as his own girlfriend is. The hot young girl isn't just a handful, she is actually fucking irritating. I'm the last affair, the sordid, nasty, futile fling, before the guy decides he never wants to stoop that low again and gets married. I am," she laughed nastily through her tears, "the Madonna to other women's Annette Bening. I just got the timing wrong with you. Sorry."

"Well even Madonna settled down eventually, didn't she? She had two babies."

"But that's terrible! Now she can't be the baby!"

"She's in her forties!"

"You're not listening to me!"

"Let me get this straight. So what you're saying is that God put you on this planet as some self-sacrificing whore of Christ to prove to straying men that monogamous relationships are more rewarding than infidelity?"

"I think so, yes," smiled Ruby, wanly.

"Bullshit! You do it because you want to." Rachel stood straight in front of her, squaring up for an imaginary playground fight. "You don't want the responsibility of a real relationship. You're afraid of needing someone. Of missing them."

"I have needed people. I need them like crazy. I've missed them, too. You don't know about my mother. You don't know about Liev."

"That's true. I know nothing about either of them. The only person I know that you know is my ex-husband."

"Okay. This kid. This dumb, invisible, shape-shifting kid called Aslan. I miss what he isn't going to let me have. I don't have anything to miss yet and that's what's killing me. My boyfriend Sebastian. When things were great between us, I missed him like crazy. When I heard he went to the Venice Film Festival to be a PA for Cameron Diaz, I thought I might die.

"Well which is it? Because my mother just died. But it was because of cancer. Not Cameron Diaz.

"My mother's dead, too. My mom was too fragile, too thin-skinned to handle life on earth, so she left it all behind. She didn't have the luxury of being a heroine to cancer. She didn't have the chance to be brave and fight it off with wit and wisdom. The thing that took her took away the wit and wisdom too, and left her not only dead, but a coward as well."

"I'm sorry. I didn't know."

"Why are you sorry? You don't like me anyway. Why would you have liked my mother? She's just like me, you know."

"I didn't *say* I would have liked her. I said that I was sorry."

"Why? Why the fuck are you sorry that my mom killed herself?"

"I think . . . I think because it probably made you how you are."

"How am I?"

"Alone."

"I *am* alone. Completely. Whereas before she died I was mostly alone. I think I prefer it this way."

"I don't think you do."

"And what makes you think that?"

"I think because you have loveless affairs with other people's husbands, for one. I think because you stagger drunk as an elephant into Madison Avenue boutiques. I think because you make yourself look so awful, so . . . ugly. If you wanted to disappear and live alone and unnoticed, you would be beautiful, as you were intended to be. You think that if you make yourself ugly enough, people will want to help you? You're being ridiculous. It doesn't work like that. Even the best-hearted people would rather be around beauty. It is the worst-hearted people who will be intrigued by you, the way you are now."

"And where is your heart?"

"My heart is in a safe-deposit box until I have further use for it. Whether you choose to be beautiful or hideous does not affect my judgment of you. If you wish me to state my camp, then so be it: I am a curious onlooker."

Twenty-four

I was there first

Placing her empty pasta bowl neatly in the dishwasher, Ruby excused herself politely and went to the bathroom. Turning the faucets on full, she leaned over the toilet bowl and started the evil orgasm. "Oh God!" she panted as the last piece of salmon fell crushed, but still pink, into the toilet. "Oh God, I'm disgusting," she breathed, pulling herself back up. Her knuckles flamed puce as she held her hands under the water. Rachel's bathroom was a temple to cleanliness. Five different facial cleansers sat on the sink and she deliberately picked the most expensive with which to wash her fingers. She took a cotton ball and patted toner across her face. When she went to the towel rack, she meant to dry her hands. But instead, she took a fluffy blue bath towel and wrapped herself in it, crouched with her back against the bathroom door. She had been there fifteen minutes when Rachel started to knock. Ruby had not bothered to lock it and her hostess let herself in, shoving Ruby into the side of the tub as she did.

Rachel crouched down beside her, then, sensing that she might be there some time, let herself lean back against the wall, too.

"Are you a drug addict, Ruby?"

Ruby shook her head.

"Are you bulimic?"

"Maybe."

"You have to stop."

"What do you know about it?"

"A lot. You want to know personal or academic?"

"Both."

"Okay. Bulimia is clearly self-loathing, but it's also quasisexual. But it's a dirty shameful Victorian brand of sexuality that is never ever erotic. You want it so bad and then you feel lousy afterward. Being bulimic is like having rough toilet sex all the time—quick, jam your foot in the door, bend over, hurry up kind of sex with no variation. No love, just a means to an end. A way to while away the time so you don't have to think about how much you hate yourself."

"I think, if it's okay with you," demurred Ruby, "that I'll be running along to bed now."

But she didn't run, she walked, very, very slowly, hoping, with each step, to feel Rachel's arms around her.

In the morning, Rachel was exhausted and Ruby was cheerful again. She tidied the kitchen, picking up the cutlery where it had been abandoned during their discussion "What are you doing?" asked Rachel through fuzzy teeth.

"Tidying! I enjoy it in other people's houses. I can make sense of other people's apartments. Just not my own.

"Uh, thank you," nodded Rachel, blearily drawing her robe tighter across her swan neck. Opening her mouth as wide as a Muppet puppet, she gave an enormous Children's Television Workshop yawn. As Rachel stretched out on the sofa, Ruby bounced around the room, before coming to rest at her feet.

"I have a question, Rachel."

"Uh-huh?" yawned Rachel, curling away from her, her whole body facing the side of the sofa.

"Tell me about your husband."

She would have sat bolt upright if she hadn't felt so tired. "Oh, come on. You knew him well enough."

Ruby shrugged her shoulders. "I fucked him. I didn't know him. I'm not really very interested in him, to be perfectly honest. I'm interested in you. So anything I want to know about Scott is in reference to you, okay?"

"Jesus, Ruby, this is all getting a little bit strange. I'm not quite sure what's going on here."

"No, neither am I. But I like you and I think you like me. I think, perhaps, we might be able to help one another."

"Perhaps."

"Listen, you know I'm screwy. Everybody knows that. But I know something not everybody knows. And that is that you're screwy too. You hold it together well, with your shiny hair and all.

It is shiny, I'm not denying it for a second. Well done. Congratulations on your hair. But it's supposed to deflect something, right?"

Rachel snorted as if this were all too ridiculous. But she could not look away from her pasty-faced interrogator.

"He did something to you, didn't he? We're friends now, Rachel. Tell me how he hurt you. Tell me what would have happened to me if I had been the one he married."

Twenty-five

Rachel's story

As Ruby set coffee and toast down in front of her, Rachel drew deep on her cigarette. The toast was burned and the coffee was too weak. Rachel almost cried then and there, for the state of the toast seemed to be an accurate representation of her, while her young house-guest's problems were encapsulated by the coffee.

Pushing the toast away, Rachel exhaled a stream of smoke, admitting with the exhalation: "He took things from me."

"What did he take?" asked Ruby, gossipy eyes agog.

"He took my curve," she answered matter of factly and stubbed her cigarette out, half-smoked, in an ashtray stolen from a Parisian bistro. "I didn't notice it at first. Until one night, five A.M., when we were lying in bed, and I happened to run my fingers across my left hip. Scott lay beside me, asleep. Valium, champagne, and Temazepam asleep. And I was awake. Coke, coke and cookies awake. Staring at the ceiling, hearing him breathing so slow, so languorously, as if he were too jaded and self-important to bother with air. Let it come to him.

"For our whole relationship, through all the ups and downs, I never allowed myself to stare at the ceiling. I've stared at the blinds, the carpet, the electrical fixtures, the en suite bathroom, and the walk-in closet. But not the ceiling. I can't look up. Whenever I look up in Hollywood, I see clouds in the shape of silicone implants and out-of-work actors. If I look up, I'll fall. I always turn on my side before I let myself do that.

"Before, when we were still on the East Coast, we'd have a fight and I would just get a cab back to my mom's. But there is no cab in the world that can give you back the last ten years of your life. Do you understand?"

"I think so."

"Look. I'm in great shape. I'm really a rather ordinary-looking woman. But I'm well turned out. I worked hard at it. From the night we married, I did five hundred sit-ups a day, starting right there in our wedding suite. Then one day I realized, staring at nobody's floor, with my everywife life, that the deep, deep curve was a straight line."

"You didn't just gain weight?"

"I don't gain weight. I don't eat." She lit another cigarette. "So I glanced at the dressing-table photos. Us at a premiere, him in Armani, me in a Dolce gown, my waist nipped in, his arm around it. I raised the duvet and looked at him. Vodka was seeping through his pores. But he was thinner, tanner, tauter than when I first met him. He looked better than ever. Tentatively, knowing already what

I would find, I dragged my palms from my ribs to my hips. The curve was gone. And I could not let him have it. So you see, in the end it really had nothing to do with you at all."

"You look curvy to me," enthused Ruby, delighted with the tale.

"You know what, honey?" laughed Rachel, stretching her hands above her head as if to emphasize the point. "I feel curvy."

Twenty-six

Critical respect

I fell in love with the kid, I really did. I worried about her right away. At first she just seems like this obnoxious little brat. But she is very fragile. I don't know what she is doing, depending upon the kindness of strangers at such a young age. That's so dangerous at the age she is, the profession that she works in. The city she lives in. There is no depending in New York and definitely no kindness. There are strangers, though. She got that part right.

Everyone always makes fun of Los Angeles. New Yorkers are so snotty about the West Coast. But you know, even though I did have my facials, my hairdresser, colorist, and masseuse, they were all good people. Good, kind souls working crappy jobs. I mean, I like to think, naive as it sounds, that I would have felt it otherwise. Bad people have vibes, like the energy left behind by dead people. I saw that masseuse twice a week. I would have known if she had been a duplicitous evil bitch. Ruby can't feel the energy from dead people because she's convinced herself that she is dead already.

Most people in California are pretty decent. I think it's because we always see such a large expanse of sky. Things fall into perspective. In New York, you barely see the sky at all, and your life becomes tinier and tinier the more you look up. You look up to the heavens for help, for salvation, but there isn't anything up there that isn't man-made, so you look back down again.

I've lived on both coasts. Ruby's worked on both coasts and that's different. She doesn't have that same intuition that I do. She gives pieces of herself away, for way below the fair price, as though her soul were a going-out-of-business sale.

It was such bad weather. And she was in such a bad state. I don't think she realizes, even now, how sick she was that first night. I mean, she was totally looped. Of course, I hated her, I was furious for the cavalier manner in which she had destroyed my marriage. But I couldn't hate her for long. First, I was worried that if I let her go home, she would die and I would have to answer a lot of police questions and the tabloids would get hold of it and it would be a big mess. And second . . . well, it sounds ridiculous . . . but this all happened right after Monica Lewinsky and Linda Tripp.

I remember being so horrified by what that woman did to that silly, skittish little girl. I promised myself that I would never be jealous or spiteful to a girl who was younger than me. Furthermore, I would take it upon myself, should the opportunity arise, to educate them in the ways of men. I still believe in a kind of emotional networking between women. As an older woman, it is my duty to give her advice, listen to her, and attempt to straighten her out, just as I would expect a woman fifteen years older than I am to advise me.

I asked her to stay the next night and she did. It turned into a week. She was in my house right through the holidays. We didn't go out on New Year's Eve. We went out the day after Christmas to buy food and toilet paper. I bought her some clothes and a toothbrush because her credit card was maxed out. She made a big deal about swearing on her life to pay me back. I don't really care. It's all Scott's money. I don't feel guilty about spending his money. It's like war reparations. He owes me serious cash for the shit he put me through.

I gave her a bunch of my own underwear. That was funny. I mean, it really was funny: this cuckold, this sex bomb, my husband's mistress borrowing my panties. I gave her the nicest ones, too. Beautiful silks and laces that Scott had bought me in France. Now why did I do that? I was being nice and I wasn't being nice. I was so relieved to be free of him and free of the struggle to be sexual and she was the one who took all that worry away for me. I wanted to be sure that when she finally walked out my front door, the lace and silk, the chore of sexual allure went with her.

I liked her right away, I really did. I liked her crazy, newborn-chicken haircut. I liked her half-moon eyebrows, stupid laugh, bitten fingernails. I liked the timbre of her voice and the way that she smelled. As screwed up as she was on all those awful pills and also, I'd guess, a good amount of alcohol, she still smelled of figs. Who smells of figs? I thought that was great! So undeserved, too! As if she'd worked out with free weights, showered, loofa'd, and scrubbed before meeting me in Prada, prearranged and in perfect time. Instead of turning up unexpected, dragging snow through the store, a wild-eyed loon with claret-stained lips.

Liking her so much, I remembered what Scott and I had in common. I remembered that we shared the same tastes. It reminded me of the times he'd bring home a couple of head shots and ask me to pick which girl would be most believable for the role of a spirited lion tamer and who would make a good suburban cheerleader with a dark secret. I knew he was fucking all of them. I knew it.

And yet my immediate, most prevalent instinct was to pick the best girl for the job. I'd pick the right girl for the part and only later I'd wonder if I'd also picked the best in bed, the hottest ass, the pertest breasts. It felt very strange. But not unpleasant. In an odd way, those were some of the times when I felt closest to Scott. He'd really listen to my choice, my reasons why a redhead could never be a believable lion tamer. I felt so close to him.

And with Ruby in my apartment and under my wing, I felt close to him again.

She asked me to help her pick a piece for an audition she had three days after Christmas. She didn't seem to me to be in any state for it. Her skin was still a wreck and she was so overexcited about the role that she was bouncing around the room, incapable of memorizing her lines. She desperately wanted to do this play off Broadway, something her agent would never have told her about, let alone let her go up for.

It was a tragicomedy the writer had penned about the film industry and he said he had created the female lead with her in mind. He had sent her a note suggesting it would be a perfect opportunity for her—"and not just in reference to the iconic bubble your agent seeks to trap you in." He said he thought she was a brilliant actress and that she reminded him of Simone Signoret. It was the French name-drop that set her off.

Although I tried to dissuade her, she insisted on reading from *Medea*.

"But it's for a part in a comedy."

"A TRAGIcomedy," she replied pointedly, obviously reading a different play from the one I had. There was a lot of swearing, falling over, drug deals gone "hilariously wrong," and some onstage sex for good measure.

"Are you sure you want to do this, Ruby? I don't even think it's that funny."

"It's not funny. That's what I keep telling you."

The day of the audition she couldn't eat, which was something of a relief because it meant she didn't throw up either. Her hair was almost all its real color, a beautiful dark brown that only made her frazzled skin look worse. We pulled on our boots and mittens and I even tied her scarf in the doorway before we rode the subway downtown. There was a man play-acting being destitute but honest and Ruby watched his performance intensely.

"Ladies and gentlemen. I am sorry to interrupt your journey. I am collecting money for babies with AIDS."

Ruby pulled out her diary and scribbled down "Babies with AIDS" in her girlish script.

"During this season of good will, please think of those less fortunate than yourselves. I am doing a sponsored walk to raise money for these helpless, afflicted babies, God's most precious gift to us: the next generation."

Ruby wrote down: "*Star Trek*."

"Please, brothers and sisters, give whatever you can to help me help those who cannot help themselves."

"Repetition," tutted Ruby.

Then he went from person to person collecting money. Some studiously ignored the man. Others gave him a dollar or two to make him go away. Ruby did not give him money and she did not ignore him either. As he held out his hand, she shook her head and loudly announced, "I'm not feeling it."

All those who had sensibly ignored him now turned her way, hissing, "Babies with AIDS!"

I hung my head in shame, staring at my reflection in my shiny leather boots. She stared fixedly ahead.

When we got out of the subway, she took my arm in hers and huddled close for warmth. Outside the theater, I asked her if she wanted me to meet her somewhere, but she told me that she wanted me to watch the audition.

Twenty-seven

Rachel loses it

"This theater looks like someone's apartment!" she exclaimed.

"Actually, it *is* someone's apartment," sneered the whey-faced director, cutting off Ruby's attempt to make small talk. "*I* live in the basement."

I guess, because of the note from the playwright, she had gone in there thinking the part was already hers. But the writer was not there and the director seemed to resent her very presence.

"Right, I can't say I know your work. I'm not familiar with my local multiplex, so do excuse me."

She did excuse him, although I wished she hadn't.

The other actresses were skinny Lower East Side types. They looked sicker—but hipper—than Ruby. Their gamine hairdos were carefully planned and paid for, unlike Ruby's which was a by-product of her instability. These were tough, happy chicks wearing weak, melancholic faces they spent hours in the mirror creating.

Thin Skin

The girl directly in front of Ruby was a hard-faced little bitch who kept staring us down. She must have been five years older than Ruby but she was wearing a pink rah-rah skirt with pale pink tights, ballet slippers, and a long-sleeved thermal vest. Her tiny breasts were braless, barely denting the fabric of her top. She wore clear lip gloss and sparkly black mascara on her enviably long lashes. She looked like Edie Sedgwick without the millions.

To match her *Medea* reading, Ruby had opted for a Maria Callas ensemble: severe red lipstick, white makeup, and cat eyeliner. She looked terrifying. So here were two girls in their twenties, going up against each other, both rocking two types of crazy.

Edie read pretty well, I'll give her that. Her set piece was well chosen, too: a monologue from *Annie Hall*. Her timing was great and I just managed to stop myself from clapping when she finished.

Ruby went on next. Under the bright lights, her makeup started to melt and leak onto her black turtleneck. She tried her best to read without looking at the page, but she still hadn't managed to memorize the lines and so she continued her performance with her eyes cast downward. Her timing was off, since she thought she was reading tragedy, and her rendition of *Medea* was hysterical; she was having hysterics, shrieking, rolling around on the floor. If she had been Björk, everyone would have called her an avant-garde genius. Instead, there was deathly silence. Ruby came down from the stage exhilarated but, seeing the director's face, her shoulders slumped. She started to say something like, "Well, thanks for the . . ." but he cut her short: "We'll call you." She had been fucked. And he never would ring her.

Edie started laughing before we were even out the door. Ruby didn't break stride. She said she wanted a sandwich and walked into a nail salon. "I mean a manicure."

"Okay, sweetheart. I'm going to buy some cigarettes. I'll be back in a minute." Then I walked back up the block to the theater and slipped in the back to find the director focused, rapt, on the fluffy waif taking the stage. Out of the corner of my eye I noticed Edie going into the toilet. I followed her in, click-clacking deliciously in my patent boots. I knew then why they had been so expensive. It was just the right tone of menace they gave off each time a heel hit the floor. I caught Edie as she came out of the stall. Before she knew what hit her, I had her shoved against the wall. I couldn't help it. I held my arm under her throat.

"I know you're just jealous because Ruby's prettier than you and a bigger star. And because she's a woman and men have to fuck you from behind so they don't have to look at your bony chest."

I heard my words reverberate off the bathroom wall and I dropped her. Dropped her! Flat on the floor! I felt like a lioness gone insane for its cub.

Then I went back to meet Ruby, pulling from my pocket the cigarettes I had had all along. She acted like she didn't give a fuck. She had her eyes closed as the girl filed her nails. She used their bathroom to wash off her crazy face. Then she went right out and bought herself a new sweater. She put on a great show, had us go out for margaritas, laughed about what had happened. I kept repeating, "Fuck 'em!" because I couldn't think of anything else to say.

Thin Skin

She said she wanted to go back to her apartment, but I made her stay with me that night. She slept in my bed with me. I cried a little onto her shoulder blade after she went to sleep. I tried really hard not to but I couldn't help it. She woke up and put her arms around me and I guess we drifted off that way.

Twenty-eight

Thank you

Rachel was . . . sweet to me. I can admit now that I was wasted when I bumped into her at Prada. I didn't know who the hell she was. I could barely remember who Scott was. The Sebastian thing was long over. Aslan didn't give a fuck. He was put off by the aura of despair that surrounded me like a force field, protecting others but not me. My heart was aching, and my belief is that when things are bad, it's better to make them worse. I just wanted to rip my heart out, throw it on the sidewalk, and stamp, stamp, stamp, until it smooshed like a water bug. I wanted to hear it squelch. If I was going to self-destruct, I wanted to watch it happen along with everyone else.

So I had been walking about thirty blocks through New York City, kicking my heart in front of me. It was snowing and of course I was crying. I was gone when she found me. It seemed so ridiculous to me that she was going on about Scott, who I never ever gave a fuck about, when I was thinking about Sebastian and how badly I'd screwed myself by letting him go. But I guess she gave a fuck about Scott. And over the course of the week I stayed with her, it started to flood back. I felt like shit. I felt like shit for what I had done to her. And I also felt physically awful. I was coming off months of Percocet, Xanax, and Valium. She weaned me off it without even meaning to. When I could see clearly I knew I wanted to be more like her. And when I could see very, very clearly, I saw through her. I saw that she was every bit as lonely as I was.

I guess I didn't notice it for a few days because she has that shiny hair and a lot of truth bounces off it. I kept asking if I could touch it. Sometimes I wouldn't even ask. I'd just reach out and pet her hair when she was on the phone or lighting a cigarette. I thought that the shininess might travel through my fingers, up my arm, and into my own head. And from my head down into my heart.

Hair comes out of your head so I do believe it is a reflection of what's inside. People with curly hair have curly thoughts and that's why it grows that way. But it is possible to double-cross your own hair follicles, *Double Indemnity*–style, until they believe themselves to be a reflection of what's inside. You can make it so. I looked through Rachel's photo albums and this woman has had the exact same hair since she was a kid. Never had bangs, never had a chin-length bob, never had a disaster with a home-perming kit, and never had it cut into a shag. Although I think Rachel is a very attractive woman, she is nowhere near as fabulous as Madonna and me. But I think she knows herself better. How can you be lonely if you truly know yourself?

Well, understanding is a lonesome place to be. When you know something about yourself and still don't act on it, you can get pretty sad. I'm lucky. I don't know myself at all. Every time I screw up, it isn't really my fault. Not really. Rachel tries so hard to be a good person. Sometimes she falls short. And those sometimes wrap around her throat like a chiffon scarf in a sports-car door.

I thought it was hilarious that she had a statue of Buddha by her bed. It was such bullshit; I had to call her on it. "Does Buddha tell you to do an hour on the Stairmaster every morning?"

She'd do her hour, take a shower and make herself a smoothie. Then she'd talk nonsense to Buddha. Then she'd lie on her bed and smoke, as if she and Buddha had just had hot sex. The cigarettes. The Buddhist shrine. The Stairmaster. The hours spent straightening her hair with a blow-dryer. If that doesn't spell lonely I don't know what does.

She told me that since Scott she had been on a few dates with a fellow Buddhist she met at yoga. He was a lot younger than her, though, and before every date she would worry that he was used to hanging around with nineteen-year-old models. All those models are Buddhists. That's how they come to work in a profession of such profound enlightenment. Yeah, I know my job is just as scuzzy, but at least my face moves when you look at it. At least I know I'm a fool.

So Rachel told me that she was really into this young Buddhist. But worrying about her weight, her wrinkles, and other people's preteens just wasn't worth it. She decided she is willing to forsake romance if it means not having to be anxious. It's the eternal choice.

Thin Skin

When she flipped out after the audition, I knew she was hiding a lot. I think she was upset as much for herself as for me. If they weren't going to be nice to me then she had to, and that's a lot of responsibility—even I can see that. I can see it, but I can't change. I felt that there was more she hadn't told me. I asked if she had ever wanted to act. She said she kind of had, that Scott had persuaded her it might be a good idea. But she wasn't any good at it so she kind of slunk back to photography. She probably didn't tell you, but after that audition we went back to her house and, before we went to bed, she took my photo for the first time. I think she was crying a little.

Twenty-nine

Fat ass

I had asked Rachel about her history with Scott so that I wouldn't have to tell her about Liev. I knew it would be a week of pain and revelation for one of us and, frankly, I'm glad it was her. I wish I had never told Scott about Liev. If I hadn't told him, I might not have begun to think that maybe it wasn't all right. Of course, I dismissed Sebastian's bombastic response almost immediately as that of an overprotective boyfriend. He was always extremely easy to dismiss, until he took my persistent suggestion and dismissed me from his life.

I didn't want to tell Rachel about Liev because I had an inkling that, though eminently sensible, she was just left of center enough to understand how much I loved him and how much he had loved me. If she had told me that I hadn't loved him—worse, that she didn't think it possible that he had loved me—I would have taken it very much to heart. If I told her about my twelfth year, she might have asked questions. Like, was it all true?

I don't know. I think so. It feels true. I need it so.

How could your parents have let it happen?

They didn't know. They couldn't have. Because if they did . . . how could they have let it happen?

If he loved you so much, how come he left without saying good-bye?

Because he did something bad. Because he would have been punished if he had stayed.

Why did you never try to find him?

I was too young. By the time I was old enough, it was too late.

Have you ever loved truly since?

I've tried to. I've even fooled myself a few times.

I would have had to tell her about Sebastian. Sebastian! A PA! A man who mopped his pizza with a paper towel so he wouldn't absorb extra grease, so his precious six-pack would remain intact. I would have had to tell her about Aslan. Aslan, for fuck's sake! Who talked to cobwebs and drank green tea. Beautiful Aslan, who bedazzled me with his pretty vacancy. Who put his fingers inside me and pulled them out knowing the truth, but wouldn't tell me what it was. I would have had to tell her about the dark inside me, how it itched and jumped and kept me up at night. I would have had to tell her that I would not listen to my mother and that all my life has been about the pursuit of beauty and the ingestion of ugliness.

Rachel said that what I needed was a roommate. The twins said they would love to have me move in with them but that it just wasn't practical. They were already cramped, what with the dogs, ferret, alligator, and iguana. I stayed a few nights on the sofa next door, but I didn't like being woken by peering dogs, sitting on my chest, staring, silent and serious, at my face.

I called Rachel back and asked if I could live with her. I thought maybe that's what she was trying to suggest and was just waiting for me to suggest it myself. But she wasn't. She said that was way too weird and could she please have her underwear back. I think most of the time Rachel forgets how and why we met. When it comes to her, it comes with a jolt that derails the train of our friendship. I know Rachel likes me, but it's just not supposed to be. That week I had with Rachel was as much of an affair—more intense, in fact— than the time I spent with her estranged husband. Only Rachel is a lot smarter than Scott is. Smart enough to let good things go before they get taken away.

A few days later, I came home to a message from Rachel, recommending Cyrinda Del'Aqua, whom she had met at a gallery opening the night before. I screwed up my nose as I wrote down the number, because I had a nasty inkling I had already met my potential roommate. I opened my eyes and she came into focus: tall, frozen mochaccino skin, long black hair piled on top of her head, faux messy, pink diamonds on her fingers, chipped red polish at the ends of them, demanding she be let into the VIP room.

Cyrinda is a downtown nightclub queen. You've read about her in Page Six. She organizes parties. People pay her to pick the venue, pick the DJ, the food, and the guest list. They pay her to make decisions. High-powered decision makers get paid high-powered money. She can pull in twenty grand for throwing a party. Her father is a

Syrian banker of huge wealth. Her mother was a second-tier sixties supermodel of immaculate WASP stock. In family photos, says Cyrinda, she and her father "look like darkies out to steal the silver."

Why the hell would she need a roommate? Despite all the money, she is a downtown girl. She likes having someone on hand to listen to her coke rants. That was the deal. She lost the lease on her fabulous SoHo loft because she was too high to bother paying the rent. Plus she needed someone to wake her up in the morning, by stroking her ear, because, she says, she "can't abide being woken by an alarm clock."

I couldn't believe Rachel thought I could possibly be a stabilizing influence on anyone.

"Listen, honey, this girl's pretty screwy. I thought it would be useful for you to realize that you're a lot saner than you think. And don't underestimate the cachet it has for her to be rooming with a movie star."

And so Cyrinda Del'Aqua moved in the next day, although she didn't treat me as if I had much cachet. Contrary to what Rachel implied, she was rich enough to know that actors are really not worthy of the tables her father gets in restaurants. I soon realized that I was to be her court jester. "Can you help me with that?" she asked, as she shook my hand, leaving her suitcase on the stoop for me to carry up the stairs.

I was so shocked that I did. When she got it into the apartment she opened it on the trundle bed I had pulled out for her and I saw that it contained almost exclusively underwear and hair accessories. "But where are your clothes?" I gasped and she frowned, "You know,

I'm really not sure. But you won't mind my borrowing yours until I get myself organized." She flung open my closet and started picking through it. I was extremely relieved to see that very little fit her and assessed that she was a good fifteen pounds heavier than I was.

"Hmm," she pouted, "this won't do. Right. I'll be back in a minute."

And she was back in not much longer than that, laden down with bags from Jeffrey's and Barney's. She spread her purchases out on the floor and shuffled them like tarot cards, arranging them over and over until she could see a meaning. "Okay!" she clapped her hands and selected a gray cashmere skirt, diamanté appliquéd Duran Duran T-shirt, leopard-print tights and Fendi high heels.

As she totaled up her purchases she said she was really embarrassed, that she wasn't usually like this.

"You're embarrassed that you spent so much?" I asked.

"No, I'm embarrassed that I spent anything at all."

What she meant was that usually all her clothes were stolen. She steals from Jeffrey's. She steals from Barney's. She steals from Saks. "I am so rich," she cheerfully confessed, "that I feel I shouldn't have to pay for anything." At her WASP houses—a compound on Martha's Vineyard, a mansion in Malibu, a London pied-à-terre, and a retreat in Connecticut—she has to wear dresses and use the correct knife and fork. She loves dressing up, wouldn't be caught dead in a pair of jeans, so the rigidity of a family dress code is not a problem for her. The knife and fork business is more problematic, since she is likely to dip her fingers in a bowl of ice cream she finds particularly enticing, rather than bothering with a spoon. At other people's dinner parties, she puts her heeled shoes on the chair-seats, not realizing that they are her host's best chairs, because to her they're really nothing.

I know she sounds unbearable. She sounds like she would have inspired Princess Margaret to class war, but her saving grace is a big one: she is fat. It sounds ridiculous, but in a world of ADBs (anorexic dumb bitches—shorthand the twins came up with) she is something of a minor heroine. Put her next to a *Vogue* cover girl, Revlon spokeswoman, ballet dancer, and *Playboy* centerfold, and she'll outshine them all. The guys love her. In a sea of ADBs, her uncontainably real DD fat-girl tits are like buoys to a drowning man.

Cyrinda is nothing like the immaculately in-condition Seurats she throws parties for. They are pointillist paintings—beautiful until you get up close and realize they're just a series of dots. "I am the opposite. You see me from a distance and think, who let in the fat girl? I'm not hugely overweight, certainly not obese. It would be no big deal, except that I love expensive clothes so much."

Clothes she can fit into if she gets the biggest size, but that stretch across her ass and thighs, wrinkling and tugging. Ignoring the tugs and wrinkles, she strokes a diamond mochaccino hand across her fat ass and drawls "Look what my father bought me at Prada!" or "Look at the shoes Marc Jacobs sent me!"

The first week she moved in with me, she wore the same thing every day. Although her shoes and T-shirts changed, the shorts and the Gucci python jacket that I had been admiring for a month always completed her outfit. It cost $4,000 so I had continued to admire it as though it were a live python in the Bronx Zoo rather than the Fifth Avenue Gucci boutique. I told her how much I loved it and that I would die to own one myself. "Ooh," she said, "buy it! Why don't you just buy it?" I couldn't answer her. There's no point trying to explain about money to people who don't think of it as a barrier.

I found myself often silent around Cyrinda, watching delightedly as she spent all morning applying her makeup, almost all of it stolen from Sephora. I put "Rio" by Duran Duran on the stereo, in order that she might have fitting musical accompaniment as she worked on her lips. She has a funny snub nose that turns up so much she can never quite close her mouth (her father's fault for insisting she get the nose job in Syria). White teeth gleaming hungry at her own reflection in the compact, she Clara Bow'd two hot-pink grooves above her upper lip. The more she went out, the more I stayed in, waiting for her to return. She invited me along, but I couldn't watch her properly in a darkly lit nightclub, with ADB chatter all around, as spiky and foolish as stiletto heels on sidewalk gratings.

When, around two or three each morning, I heard her key in the door, I would tap on the partition and join her as she kicked off her pumps and crawled, fully clothed, under the covers. Yawning, she'd précis her night, reeling off a list of who showed and who didn't, who dazzled and who made a fool of themselves, who was asked to dance by DiCaprio, and who was caught giving a blow job in full view of the entire room.

Her mochaccino jaw would be grinding and she'd waver between party fatigue, dragging sleepy-time oxygen through her upturned nose, and the desire to sit up and talk. She'd turn away from me, her face burrowed into the pillow, her hair billowing about her like Prada ribbons on a Marc Jacobs maypole. Then she'd sit bolt upright, tucking pillows behind her back, holding her face with her hand so she could have perfect eye contact. She liked to control things. I liked to be controlled.

"Be a honey and get me a bowl of cereal. Make sure the milk is nice and cold and that the bowl is filled to the top." And I'd do it immediately, balancing the brimful bowl with utmost attention, all the while trying to maintain eye contact so that she wouldn't turn over and slump into sleep. Taking the bowl from me, she shoveled spoonfuls of cereal past her still-glossy lips, timing the spoon so it would avoid the chomps of her coke-stimulated teeth. Chomp and chomp and spoon and swallow. Chomp and chomp and spoon and dribble. Bored of a bite, I'd have to remind her the food was still on her tongue, as she recalled the electric-blue jumpsuit worn by Leo's lady friend.

I thought about the girls I was usually put up against in auditions. In L.A., they were slim as pins with soft, fat lips. In New York they were even thinner, with lips to match (which is the New York India scene's notion of anti-L.A. elegance: thin lips). Cyrinda was lucky that she considered acting so lowly. If she had ever had to put herself through auditions, her belief in her own infallible beauty would have been considerably knocked.

She *was* gorgeous, touchable. I caught her touching herself once or twice, sometimes in masturbatory poses, sometimes just running a finger across her soft forearm, smiling at the high-quality silk that kept her insides from falling out. It was as if her impossibly rich family had opted for the most expensive materials when conceiving of Cyrinda. It is not just a healthier diet and standard of living that makes rich people appear prettier than poor people. Their parents spend more on them. Her parents knew, perhaps, that they were going to divorce while their baby was learning to toddle, and they wanted to make up for emotional trauma by swapping it for looks, no expense spared.

The first thing that you see about Cyrinda is her skin. Like Marilyn with self-confidence, she has flesh impact. But before you see her, the first thing you smell about Cyrinda is that she never showers. Nobody minds because she is so rich and she smells of the dirt that lines paper money, not the dirt of the streets or the farm. Because she is so rich and so popular, nobody says anything.

Nobody tastes it when they kiss her or go down on her, because they will not allow themselves to. Her popularity is there, so her smell is not. They do not see the visual side effects of her money dirt. There's dirt under her nails and mascara collecting in the corners of her eyes. Men have mentioned that, the nail filth and eyelash gunk, but only in the context of its being attractive. They say she is the filthy girl made flesh.

If I were a guy, and I had no nose, I would want to screw Cyrinda.

Many have, although it has never altered her continuing appeal to those who have yet to give it a try. She is the only woman I have ever encountered whose sexual exploits are, like men's, celebrated rather than frowned upon.

She wears a different vintage top every single night and the same shorts. Not a version of the shorts but the same pair. It was a few days into her residency on Bleecker Street that I noticed strange stains at the bottom of them. The more disgusted I became by her, the more I wanted to look at her. And the more I wanted to look at her, the more I wanted to touch her.

The twins thought she had rad style. They liked that she was fat. They loved her crazy, bird's-nest hair and vintage T-shirts. But they didn't like her voice. They didn't like the way she talked to me or the way that I responded.

"That girl is so fucking arrogant," hissed the red twin, cornering me at the laundromat. "I mean, she has got great clothes. Good taste. *For a rich person.*"

"So what's the problem?"

"She fucking stinks, for one thing."

"What are you talking about?"

"Oh come on, Ruby, I can smell her from across the street. And you can too. So tell me. Do you like her for her T-shirts? Or for her money? Because I can understand wanting a roommate who has good clothes you can borrow. But if it's money, then that's just dumb 'cause you made your own already. All by yourself."

"My parents had money, I'm sorry to tell you."

"Yeah. But you didn't take any of it. You made it all yourself. Why is this girl so arrogant? Who is she to judge you? As far as I can see, all she does is swan around being fat with a credit card."

"What is so wrong with that?'

"It *is* wrong. You know it's wrong. Not for her. That's probably the best her she can be. But it's wrong for you."

Cyrinda went to a gallery opening that night, followed by a dinner in honor of someone at Miramax. It was funny that she was invited and I wasn't. I made that studio money last year. But I guess a year is a long time ago. She had never made them any money, but she had never stopped having it either.

When she came home, she was so fucked up she tripped over the humidifier. I opened the door to see what was happening, and water from the tank was sliding across the floor, where the wood tiles tipped. She had managed to find her way to the bed, but only to the very edge of it. She was lying face down, with her head and torso falling over the side. Mustering more strength than I had bothered to use since the last time there was no one around to unscrew the top from my marmalade, I rolled her over onto her back. In doing so, I placed her closer to the center of the bed.

"Mmmlaghpersatma."

I knew, even half conscious, that Cyrinda was issuing an instruction, so I leaned in above her lips, as though straining to hear the final words of a dead person.

"What was that you asked?"

She opened one eye and answered, clear as a bell, "LIE BESIDE ME."

Chided, I leapt onto the bed beside her, at which she groaned, "Jesus, go easy on me. I've had a bit of a night."

"Sorry."

"That's okay," she whispered and turned away from me.

We lay there for some time, her breathing heavy toward the wall, me flat on my back, staring up at the ceiling. An hour passed, and she never turned back toward me. A little chilly over the covers, I inched closer toward her for warmth, snuggling up against her back. She was fast asleep, the deep, true sleep of the genuine hedonist. Her hair, unclipped in places, was falling down her back like plush rats' tails. Fox tails. Mink tails. Cyrinda wore her fur proudly, answering my criticism of her latest purchase with, "But this is Gaultier!" as if that overruled any notion of animal rights.

I put a hand at the crown of her head, and followed the dark strands down to her shoulder blades, one of the only sharp areas on her otherwise soft body. I walked my fingers up the back of her T-shirt to her bra strap and felt, with my thumb, its texture against her skin. I moved up to her neck, pulling aside her hair like a dark velvet curtain. Beneath the dark velvet was crème-brûlée silk. And beneath the crème brûlée was, I supposed, blood and other slimy things, although I could hardly imagine it. I saw her getting harder the further into her body one traveled because Cyrinda was an inside-out crab, with all the delicious, soft meat on the outside and nothing you would want near you underneath.

A car skidded outside. I waited for it to hit a tree, but it didn't. And because the car and its driver escaped unscathed, I decided it would be okay for me to proceed along her body. Slipping my arm around her broad rib cage, I started stroking her breast. I was so scared, I didn't know if it was her left or right breast, or even if it was a breast, only that it was flesh. I did it very lightly at first as if it were a mistake. I kept going, like a dirty old man on the subway, holding my breath, waiting for her to shout, "Pervert!" Am I still in the shape of a beautiful girl? I asked myself. Touching another beautiful girl, needing her lush prettiness, am I still pretty, if I need it so badly?

As if in answer, Cyrinda stirred. I sensed her eyelids flutter open. But she didn't say anything, so I kept stroking. I waited for another car to zoom past the window, but there was no sound, except us: her breathing hard, me breathing soft, too scared to breathe properly in case I made too much noise. It felt like we were alone in the city. She turned to face me, her beautiful bunny face inquisitive.

"Were you doing what I think you were doing?"

"Yes."

"Good. I liked it. Don't stop."

As soon as she said that, I couldn't do it anymore. I withdrew my hand so fast; she might have been about to bite it. I nursed it as though she had bitten me, holding it to my mouth until, stirred to action, she sat up straight, took my hand and, holding it behind my back, kissed me on my bitten lips. There was so little love to the kiss she gave me that I wanted to give it back.

But I had started something that she seemed to think was a terribly good idea, because now she wouldn't let me stop. The more she kissed me, the less I wanted it. I realized too late that I want to admire and even touch beauty, but not to taste it. Because, as I should have known, from everything I already knew about her, beauty tastes filthy. When she slid down my body and, with the disinterest of someone who had done it a hundred times before, began to unhook my underwear with her thumbs, I had to push her head away.

"As you like it," she snapped, and, turning her back on me

again, pulled herself back under the covers and, within seconds, feigned loud snores, all the more discourteous for their voluminous fakery. If I slept with someone with fake tits I think I would just find it rude. Like, do they think I'm that dumb? Big spherical balloons jutting from their rib cage? Cyrinda's snores sounded like fake tits.

Thirty

I invented Russell Crowe

The next morning she was up and out uncharacteristically early. She had no office to go to, so she occupied her "business hours" pounding the streets, cafés, flea markets, and boutiques of the city, venturing out to Brooklyn and Queens to work the charity stores there if she was feeling particularly productive. Discovering a batch of boy-sized Bowie T-shirts gave her a warm feeling of achievement that provided her with a week of well-being and self-worth. All her business was done over her cell phone and she had a knack of taking stunningly personal calls during business meetings and long business calls during evenings in front of the video.

She was not a stupid woman and yet there was absolutely no point in lending her your favorite book or inviting her to watch your favorite video with you, since she would talk all the way through either. In a pure party environment she passed for charming, chatty, and vibrant. In daylight-hours scenarios where she was required to be still in her own body, she came off as absolutely crazy because she couldn't even read a magazine article, let alone a novel, without having someone to talk to while she did it.

She didn't come home that night, nor the next. Within days I noticed that, little by little, her clothes were being moved out. I feel so depressed by gradual falling-outs, where the person and their life float away from you piece by piece like luggage from a shipwreck. I would much prefer the friendship to go down with the boat than to float with the luggage, washing up eventually on a remote island where no one would find it but where it would still exist.

Just as I was wondering how to get her out completely as soon as possible, my thoughts were distracted by the sight of a large cockroach, dead and decaying, smack in the middle of a glue trap at the base of the bathroom sink. I decided not to wait in for her and scanned the papers for movie programs. Pulling on a pair of flip-flops, I got the hell out of there.

I stood in line to see *Gladiator,* more distraught than I was when I bolted out of the house, because the line was so long. I think I have a reverse version of the Cassandra syndrome. You know? She could see into the future but her curse was that no one would ever believe her. My curse is that everyone believes me. Of course, I don't foresee wars or plagues, just pop stars and movie idols. As soon as I started saying that there was this great Australian character actor named Russell Crowe, he becomes the world's biggest star. When I'm out there, busily collecting rare B-sides by an indie band called R.E.M., they sign to a major label and become the biggest rock act in the world. It's at a point where I'm scared to like anything for fear that they'll become huge. Sliced up and handed to the people in such slim portions that there's nothing left for me.

As the line grew longer behind me, I tried to swallow my panic. Everyone around me was talking about how Russell Crowe is absolutely their favorite actor and I just wanted to cry. I was wearing the same pajamas I had had on for two days and nights. They weren't even cute, attention-seeking pajamas with blue flannel sheep, or a sexy negligée, underwear as outerwear. I had on a pair of ratty track pants and an oversized T-shirt I bought on St. Mark's Place that says "I love chicks with big tits." I bought it for Sebastian who thought it was totally punk-rock and cool. On me, with my breasts bursting through the print, it was just alarming. The track pants had pieces of cord digging into my stomach and they were hell to sleep in but I was too lazy to take them off. The outfit I had on was special, in that it was appropriate neither for the comfort of my bed nor for public viewing.

Of course the man I wanted very least to be viewed by was in front of me on the escalator as I made my droopy way to theater three. Sebastian had his arm around a statuesque Asian girl, but when he realized it was me, he quickly dropped his arm to his side, as though caught out. We reached the top of the stairs and the Asian statue stood dopey at his side, until he gave her a little shove in the direction of the popcorn stand. I kept turning my head to catch secret glances at us, glances that were about as subtle as my T-shirt. Steering me against a wall holding a poster of Angelina Jolie's giant eye and mouth, he ignored the T-shirt. He's a man so I knew he was thinking I had it on because it was something he had worn. He was right.

"How have you been?" asked Sebastian. "How are you?"

I considered the question. "I'd quite like to die," I stated matter of factly as if picking fluff from a sweater.

"What's wrong?"

No casual small talk with this ex-girlfriend, I made damn sure of that. "There was a cockroach in my bathroom. A big one." Out of the corner of my eye, I saw the statue teeter toward us, popcorn and soda in hand.

"And you couldn't catch it?" asked Sebastian, studiously ignoring her.

"No, I did catch it. It was caught, dead in the sticky trap at the base of the sink. I noticed when I went to brush my teeth."

"So it was dead?"

"Yes."

"And it was in a trap."

"Uh-huh."

"So what was the problem?"

I sighed as if he were the stupidest man on earth, which is how I always treated him even at the very apex of our love affair. "The problem is that it was there."

"And that makes you want to die because . . . ?"

"Because I didn't want it to be there."

"Right. Um, we're all going to see *Gladiator,* I guess." He finally acknowledged the statue who, eyeing me quickly, smiled weak as a cup of chamomile tea. "Why don't you sit with us?"

I thought about it for a moment, breathing through my nose as I imagined sitting on one side of Sebastian with his lady friend on the other. A tear trickled down my cheek, as expected yet unedifying as sweat on the back of a go-go dancer. I started to sob.

"I can't watch this film. I can't watch this film."

A nice old lady on her way into the theater stopped to offer me a Kleenex.

"Fuck you! Fuck you! I loved him first. I loved him, you bunch of sheep motherfuckers! Have you seen *Proof*? Have you seen *Romper Stomper*? Hands up anyone here who has seen *Virtuosity*? I didn't think so."

There was spit flying out of my mouth as I screamed, "Fuck you all!"

That's when Security removed me, dragging me down the escalator adjacent to the one I had just glided up.

Thirty-one

Get me out of here

Someone had recognized me and called the *Enquirer,* who had a photographer waiting to snap a photo as Security threw me out on the sidewalk. I couldn't help but stop crying as they then turned around and began roughing up the photographer too. Swallowing the desire to kick the photographer in the ribs, Sebastian, thinking fast for once, grabbed the camera. "I'll press charges," shrieked the paparazzo.

The taxi pulled jerkily away from the cineplex, Sebastian holding my head on his shoulder, the statue stranded streets behind us.

"Holy shit!" screamed Sebastian, stuffing the film in his blazer pocket.

I was laughing hysterically. "That was brilliant! That was fucking brilliant. That guy will press charges. You're going down, Sebastian Chase. Lawsuit!" My panic ignited again by the word "lawsuit," I switched back from laughter to tears, realizing, in seven-second time delay, that I was no longer laughing but sobbing.

"Ruby. Calm down. Chill the fuck out. What is it? What are you really upset about?"

I saw the driver glance in his rear view mirror, not as if he were worried about having a psycho in his car, but as if he really wanted to know what I was really upset about, too.

"I'm upset about Russell Crowe being successful. I mean, okay, he's allowed to be successful. He's allowed to be an in-demand character actor. But he wasn't supposed to be a leading man. I never said he could be a romantic lead. I NEVER SAID THAT WAS ACCEPTABLE. Nobody asks me anything."

The driver and Sebastian rolled their eyes. "I'm going to ask you again. What are you really upset about?"

"I'm upset," I choked, "because there is a cockroach in my bathroom."

"Really?" demanded Sebastian.

"Really," I answered, my voice as sloppy as my own melted-caramel eyes. I often think my whole life, my whole world, would be completely different if only I had blue eyes. It would be completely better, which is what we mean when we use the phrase "completely different."

"I'm sorry, Ruby, but I don't understand what's so awful about a dead cockroach."

My voice was now flat with disgust. "I hate ugly things. That's why I hate myself."

"Ruby, for the last time, you're fucking beautiful."

"That's very sweet of you to say." Ricky Martin was on the radio. He was segueing between two languages, making no sense in either of them. "That cockroach looks how I feel. I think my worst fear is of it crawling on me, crawling on my feet or on my face. Because then how I feel on the inside would be on the outside too."

Sebastian shook his head, the muscles in his thick neck bulging. "I don't understand what's going on. I don't understand why you're so unhappy." He fumbled in the pocket of his faded denim jacket for a cigarette.

"No. You never did. And I will always love you for it."

Assuring him that I was okay now, I hugged him good-bye outside my apartment. He took a few steps toward the curb before turning back to me. I was fumbling with my key, trying to breathe through my nose, determined to let him walk away.

"Ruby, do you want me to come and get rid of the cockroach?"

"Yes! Yes!" I almost cried with relief. And then I did cry with relief. He carried me up the stairs and placed me on the bed. Looking at the Gucci/Prada debris scattered around what was once the front room, he asked if someone had moved in. The clothes Cyrinda had left behind were so expensive you couldn't really tell if they were for a boy or a girl because they were too avant-garde. Because he wasn't sure what was going on, he wasn't quick enough to mask his jealousy that I might be living with another man. Too tired to lie, I told him about Cyrinda. Later he asked me when I got a roommate and where she slept.

"On the trundle bed, of course."

"There is no trundle bed."

The silly bitch had taken the dumb cot and left behind her $4,000 Gucci python jacket.

Thirty-two

The bug man

He undressed me, running his long fingers along my soft flesh. Then he opened the closet door he had seen me open scores of times but had never opened himself, and found a pair of pajamas. Real pajamas, that he had given me, soft blue flannel from Macy's. I slid the pants over my pale legs. He pulled the top across my shoulders, buttoning it up, closing it across my tummy and above my breasts and away from the sexual tension that lingered beside the tears and terror, like a guest reluctant to leave a party despite the hosts' protestations that they want to go to bed.

He pulled the duvet up to my nose, having wiped it of snot with his freshly ironed handkerchief. Then he flicked on the bathroom light and surveyed the root of the problem.

I watched from my bed as Sebastian bent down onto the tiles, dirtying his crisp chinos, and scooped up the cockroach, encased in its black glue coffin, into a wad of toilet paper. For a moment he held the off-white wad as if it were a Dickensian knapsack bearing all his worldly possessions. Then he tossed it into the trash and, smiling, placed his hands on my shoulders.

"Don't touch me!" I screamed. "You touched a cockroach!"

"I didn't touch a cockroach!" he protested. "My fingers never touched it, or the glue trap." He wiggled his fingers in front of my face. "See, silly girl? I didn't let it infect me."

My tears stopped. My face fell. "You have to leave now."

When I woke up the next day, I pulled on a pair of sunglasses I had bought for $199 and went across the street to buy a breakfast cupcake. Digging in my pockets, I scraped together my pennies to make the dollar-fifty price.

Cupcake in hand, I stormed back to my apartment to begin my cupcake ritual. It doesn't taste good unless you tear at it the right way. If you just bite it, the cake tastes like what it is: eggs, sugar, flour, butter. But if you tear the cupcake apart at just the right angle, you unleash a culinary atom bomb with a pleasantly soothing effect. If you eat the cupcake by chomping right into it, you just feel fat. Eat it right and you get the Valium effect—you still feel fat but you also feel numb and sleepy. Cheaper than John, I laughed.

Of course I don't actually laugh out loud, which I guess means it isn't that funny. And if it isn't that funny, it must be sad. So I start crying. Probably for the second time that morning. I lose track. It's been so long since I've had a day without tears. Until recently, though, they mostly hit around five o'clock.

I looked in the mirror. I heard Cyrinda come in, but my eyes didn't move from the mirror. I turned the medicine cabinet upside down trying to find a razor. There was only a dirty Bic and I couldn't get the safety guard off. I had to cut the plastic with a pair of toenail scissors. The banality of self-hatred is perhaps the most alarming thing about it. This razor, I think, looking at it as intently as I had my own reflection, is supposed to make me prettier, more touchable, so that I will not disappoint or disgust a man who deigns to fuck me.

Bending a segment of razor at a right angle, I drew it across my throat. Not deep enough to die, but deep enough to bleed fast enough to match my tears. Then I lay back on my bed and listened to John Coltrane, trying to hear the pattern, falling into sleep as the answer came to me, leaving just as fast when my first snore showed it the door. The cut crusted over with blood and the stream stopped, trapped inside me.

I felt sorry for my blood. It is trapped inside me. No way out, no polite excuse to go, circling and circling laps on my body. Sometimes I felt it speeding up its circuit just to relieve the monotony of Ruby legs, Ruby arms, Ruby toes and fingers. That's when I feel it, there in my extremities. It kicks at the circuit. But I feel nothing in my brain or my heart anymore. The extremes are well nourished but the vitals are dead.

Thirty-three

The morning after

When I woke up the next morning, I knew exactly what I had done the night before and raced straight to my vantage point at the bathroom mirror to admire my handiwork. The cut was, as I had suspected it might be, graphically effective, although it stung somewhat more than any of the cuts I had ever made in my arms, tummy, or legs. This was new ground for me and I wanted everyone to see it. If I wanted someone to see the arm cuts, I had to pretend I really didn't want them to and then casually, and to their loudly voiced horror, let a long sleeve slip just so. The cut on my neck was not disguisable, even pretend disguisable, since the only option was a turtleneck and it was sweltering outside.

Tiptoeing through the front room, I found Cyrinda passed out in a pile of her own clothes. I guess it wasn't working out with whoever she had decided to move on to. She woke as I opened the door and I heard her call out, "Seeya later, honey!" in the cheery slang of those who know they have behaved badly, but I was gone.

Calmed by my excellent cut, I went to see *Gladiator*. The theater was almost empty save for a few blue-rinse pensioners who had no idea who Russell Crowe was ("He's that British guy, right, Herb?" and "He's Richard Burton's son" were two inventions I heard loudly whispered during the film). Despite the talking, their lack of appreciation for Russell meant that I enjoyed myself tremendously.

Buoyed, I went to see Sebastian at work. He had been installed in an office while his new client tried to set up a production company. He was just leaving his desk for lunch when I made it to the top of his third-floor walk-up. "Jesus, Sebastian! I thought you were supposed to be a high-powered PR. It's got to be ninety degrees outside. Do you think you could move to a building with an elevator? And proper air conditioning, maybe?"

"What the fuck have you done to your neck?" he screamed.

"When are you going to fix the air conditioner?" I asked again, softly, as though he had said something rude I was going to rise above by ignoring.

Dragging me by the arm, he pulled me into his office, closing the glass door behind him. I waved merrily at his coworkers, who looked on aghast as Sebastian shook me by the shoulders. I had fully intended to cry for him, and my eyes were just working up to it, when he derailed my train of thought by breaking down in tears himself. Tentatively, I touched his shoulder, but he flicked me away.

"I'm sorry," I said.

But his shoulders were heaving now.

"I'm sorry. I said I'm sorry! I won't do it again! Please just stop crying."

"I can't just stop crying, you stupid, selfish bitch. I don't understand how this can be. You're not in my life, but you're still ruining it."

"Hang on, it's my body."

"But you did it to hurt me."

"I did not do it to hurt you." I thought about this and amended my defense. "I showed you to hurt you."

"Yeah, well it worked." Collecting himself, he pulled a handkerchief from his pocket, wiped his face and clenched his jaw.

Checking past my head, to his colleagues on the other side of the window, he saw they had forgone lunch in order to follow our soap opera. Keeping his voice at an even tone, his mouth barely moving, he hissed, "You're making me fucking crazy. Wherever you go, your problems overflow onto whoever is in the vicinity at the time."

"You're just cross because you loved me so much. And now it's finished and we didn't get married or have babies or live happily ever after."

"I never thought we'd have babies. You're the baby . . ."

"Yeah, I know, but that doesn't change how much you loved me. I know what makes you try not to think about me, because the same things keep me awake at night too. You wonder, if we're not together now, what happens to love left in the past? Where does it end? Did it fall into the earth and fertilize your new life? I'm sorry you loved me so hard. I'm sorry I didn't love you back in a way that could have made sense to you. But I did love you."

He sharpened a pencil on his desk that was already sharp as a punchline and, without looking at me, said, "You have to get help."

"I want help." Until I said it out loud, I didn't realize quite how much I did. I knew I cried and wailed and prayed to a God I didn't believe in to help me with problems I didn't believe I had. But once I heard the request in my own voice, calm and collected, unfettered by drama-class weeping, directed at something other than my own reflection, I knew it was a real plea and not just a catchphrase.

Sebastian seemed just as taken aback because, laying down his pencil, he folded his hands across his knees like a public schoolboy reprimanded and replied, "I can't help you."

"Thank you," I said, "thank you," and walked out of his office and back down the stairs, with what little grace I could muster, not complaining about the heat, although this time I actually felt it.

Cyrinda was still asleep when I put my key in the door. I glanced around the corner at the answering machine, willing the light to flash with someone, anyone who could help me. If it were a telephone company salesman living inside the red blink, I would have rung him back. But the only thing flashing was my heart, flicking silently on and off, jam-packed with hundreds of messages I didn't want to hear and hadn't bothered to listen to in months. If I could have had a better understanding of my own body, if I'd had the patience to figure out where my heart was plugged in, I would have yanked it right out of the socket.

But I remembered, of all the classes I never paid attention to in school, biology was the one I went out of my way to block completely. I mapped out my emotional fate then, when I decided that it was too frightening to try to understand how one's own body functions. Because if you know how it works then it is not too hard to figure out how it can fail. And the best way to pretend you don't know you're failing is to pretend you don't know you are competing. When people are vocally modest, you can tell they're very frightened. For "What, me, little old me? No one is interested in little old me" delete and read "Why is nobody interested in little old me? Am I really so little? How do I get big? Wait, let me cover my ears, I don't want to know."

I told myself that if I went out tonight, and if I was recognized by a fan, I would ask them to help me, or try to. But then it struck me that people who ask for autographs are very rarely fans and very rarely interested in the celebrity they're requesting a part of. Because they don't really want anything to do with the individual. What the fan wants is celebrity the entity, the whole messy cloud, which hovers above New York City like a spaceship.

"Take me!" people plead to the ship. "Prod me! Probe me! Pick me, motherfuckers!"

But the spaceship just sits there.

Thirty-four

Last chance

As luck would have it, no one recognized me in any of the four bars I hopped. It's like wanting to find a boyfriend—you never get one when you're looking. And because I wanted so desperately to be looked at that evening, everyone turned their eyes away. The last bar I hit was on Ludlow Street. As I walked over some gratings, the sound of the keyboard surged dully beneath me. I sat across the street and smoked a cigarette. I prayed to my mother and got a couple of drinks. There were streaks of hot pink tearing strips out of the sky as the sun began to set. Aslan appeared. I didn't recognize him at first, out of context. I pictured a makeup girl blotting his forehead with powder as he fumbled for his Marlboro, and it made me gasp. I settled my bill and followed him across the street and down the stairs.

He told me what I needed to know. I hurried home to get on with it.

Thirty-five

Bad roommate

Cyrinda was not there when I got home, although she had taken the Cinnamint toothpaste that I thought was now mine by default. There is no default with Cyrinda. She had taken other things that were mine too. A bottle of my bubble bath, a tube of scarlet lipstick she had been coveting.

I took fifty pills from a jumbo bottle of aspirin. I laid them out on my desk and popped them in my mouth one by one. Om. Yum. Good girl, Ruby. I drifted into unconsciousness, calm and content, because I was doing the right thing.

"Listen," whispered the thought of suicide, which was lying beside me with its arm around my torso.

"Uh-huh," I answered dreamily, letting it nuzzle my neck, grateful, at last, for contact, even if it was not human.

"Listen," elaborated the thought of suicide, "Liev wants to talk to you."

Thirty-six

The other side

The ambulance man kept prodding my arms to keep me awake. Irritated not so much that I was still alive, but by all the screaming going on around me, I closed my eyes and went back to the other side for another forty winks.

Thirty-seven

Sebastian works it out

I floated back up to the surface to find myself in a hospital bed with tubes in my nose and something sticking into the back of my hand. A male nurse was standing over me and asking, scar by scar, in a heavy Indian accent, "Is this recent? Is this recent?"

"That one?" answered Sebastian helpfully. "I haven't seen that one before. Oh, that one on her upper arm is at least a year old."

"Why you do this?" asked the nurse cheerily. "You won't be pretty for husband."

"I'm not terribly concerned with prettiness," I replied sternly. The first living words out of my dead-asleep mouth, they worked their way up my throat past phlegm soaked in black calcium.

"Bullshit!" laughed Sebastian, squeezing my hand.

"No. Beauty, I'm obsessed with. Ugliness too. But what the hell s pretty? Who could possibly be interested in that? Doesn't it sug-est," I paused because my throat was raw from the tubes that had been shoved down there to pump my stomach, "the desire to please? Have I ever, as long as you have known me, exhibited any desire to please anyone except myself?"

"No," he said solemnly. "I guess that's why you're here."

He pulled up a chair and sat beside me. He traced, with his eyes, the tubes in my nose, the tube in my hand, adding, as best he could, a protective force field to the ones in plastic, already in place. I knew what he was doing, even if he didn't, and I was grateful for his effort.

"Sebastian," I breathed, "I love you."

"I love you too," he answered, although I could tell, in a flash, that he no longer did.

When, standing by my ER bed, Cyrinda and Sebastian were told that I would pull through with no physical damage, they both left, Cyrinda to attend a party at Lot 61 and Sebastian anywhere at all, so long as it was the hell away from me, forever and ever amen. Though their destinations were different, Cyrinda and Sebastian opted to share a cab and clung to each other within moments of the ride. When Cyrinda got out at Lot 61, so did Sebastian, determining, correctly as it happened, that that was the last and final stop on the "Away From Ruby" bandwagon.

Thirty-eight

Eastern European irritation

I was transferred from ER to the intensive care unit, where I was put on constant, around-the-clock watch. The first six hours a middle-aged Polish lady sat on a chair by the foot of my bed and watched me sleep, watched me breathe, watched me joylessly consume a packet of saltines and a bowl of tomato soup. I felt pangs of middle-class guilt as I tried to work out how much she might be getting paid to stop the princess from doing it again.

"Hey, Daddy, I wanna pony! I wanna go to Miami! I wanna bracelet from Tiffany! Hey, Daddy, I wanna die! Hey, everybody, watch me die! Ya ready?" On tiptoes, tan legs, white bathing suit, no breasts yet, forcing everybody to watch a fairly ordinary dive. "Did you see it? Did you see me dive?"

Did you see me die? Did you see me die? Are you watching?

The sense of profound irritation I felt transcended the period of spiritual questioning one expects to enter following an unsuccessful suicide attempt.

"Why can't I even go to the bathroom without you watching me?" It was the first question I asked of her and the first answer she gave me. With less of an accent than I had expected, but with much stronger anger, she said, "You know why."

"No—" squealy, squealy princess voice "—I don't . . . oh, wait. Yeah, okay," I conceded, "I know," although until just then I *had* quite forgotten ". . . but listen, it didn't work and so I'm not going to do it again, am I?"

"We don't know that."

In "we" I saw not the hospital establishment, the doctors and nurses on the emergency ward, but a phalanx of middle-aged Polish ladies, watching me from every angle.

"Oh come on. Any sensible person must know that it's too grand a gesture to fail at and then immediately attempt again. You're missing the point." I looked at her. "Or maybe you're getting the point and I'm missing it completely. Forget about it. You can watch me pee."

At that, she turned her back.

Thus reprimanded, I crept back into bed and, pulling myself under the covers so my head was covered too, I pretended to go to sleep. Soon I was asleep. When I woke up, it was late at night or early in the morning and the lady was gone. In her place sat a withered white nun. She was staring at me, or attempting to. Her eyes were unfocused, tripping her up somewhere in the middle distance.

There was a beatific smile on her splotchy face. There was a sweet smell in the room that wasn't sweets and wasn't goodness either. It was bourbon. The nun was drunk. As she registered me, I tried to pretend I was not awake, but winking at me, she cooed, "Ahm praying for you, little girl."

She didn't look like she was praying.

She tilted forward in her chair. "Are you a good Christian girl?"

"No," I answered, peering grumpily out from the corner of my sheet, "I'm a good Jewish girl."

"What's that?" she asked, although I knew, from the way her red ears perked up, that she had heard me perfectly well the first time.

"I said, I'm Jewish. Sorry I can't be of more use to you."

She moved toward my bed. I thought, in a moment of sheer terror, that she was going to strangle me with her bony hands for murdering our Lord Jesus Christ. But, leaning into my face, she whispered, so the bourbon on her breath stung my eyeballs, "Then you are my cousin. And ahm praying for you hard!"

The day passed as had the previous one: saltines, soup, and staring. I was unhappy when I realized I was awake because I was so worried that I would have to look at the nun—worse still, talk to her. Unable to keep my eyes from opening any longer, I raised myself up onto my haunches and let the lids spring open, preparing myself for the worst.

Thirty-nine

Ethnic wisdom

Sitting in the staring chair was an African-American lady of considerable age and girth. She was not staring at me. She was doing her knitting, pulling together a scarf in tones of aubergine and pink. Aubergine and pink! Side by side in sweet harmony! Her face was generous, so I knew that she was not making the scarf for herself. But, glancing at her clothes, yellow, green, and orange, I saw the taste was her own and that the scarf would be appreciated by her and her alone. "Um, thank you," some disappointed kid would stammer and the maker would never, ever know it wasn't the kid's best gift ever.

Seeing me watching her, not bothering to watch me, I was pleased when she did not act as if she had been caught out.

"Well, good morning, girl who does not love her own life! Today you will learn to love it!"

"What is happening today to make me love life so much?" I asked nervously, my tummy rumbling in support of my anxiety.

"Today you meet Jesus!"

My eyes burst wide in my slack gray skin. "What are you saying? Am I going to die? Will I not pull through? The doctor said I was fine." I started to cry, sorry, sorry, sorry for what I had done, wanting it to become undone as much as I had once wanted to be famous.

"What you talk about, chile? Of course you going to live. You be alive until he come to take you. No choice in it for you. Today he is stopping by to remind you of that. It is not in your hands, chile, so just you lay back and relax."

Embarrassed and a little angry, I dried my eyes on the back of the hand that didn't have a broad bandage, from where a tube had been detached as I slept. No tube and no sense of humor.

"Should you be saying all this? I mean, isn't this against hospital policy or something? Why am I being indoctrinated?"

I imagined my new life as a terribly serious person, easily offended but, unlike in the past, offense acted on, rather than forgotten in the glint of a hot-fudge sundae.

"What you mean, indoctrinated?" she frowned, jabbing the air with her knitting needle, the aubergine and pink work done, flying from the needle like the official flag of the psychiatric ward. God bless this psychiatric ward, home of the gibbering, land of the nervous, hand on heart, stand up tall. I am very brave when I am completely alone.

"There was a nun here last night, talking about God."

"That ol' fool"

"You're calling God a fool?" I gasped, intrigued.

"No, chile, I callin' that old fool a fool. She don't got no brains in her head, going around gettin' drunk and then assaultin' patients with prayer. She make God sound like a man rubbin' up against you on a crowded subway."

Her name was Marcelle, just as it ought to have been. Delighted, I forced myself properly awake, pulling on the smiley foam slippers the hospital had left by my bed, and walked over to peer out the window. New York was shining in the heat, all rude, and I was glad that I was not down there in it, but that I could watch it from a sanitized perch. We were on the tenth floor and, gazing down, I watched the streets filled with people who had not tried to kill themselves. They had tried, and were still trying, with tremendous effort and strain, to live.

They were the ones who had to be in the hundred-degree heat, on filthy streets, sneering and spitting at each other, the spit sizzling on the sidewalke like hatred. That was their reward. Rich people rent apartments that are high up and have huge windows so that they can look down and get a clear view of just how dismal it is not to be extremely wealthy.

"If this were a room in an apartment complex, it would go for $3,000 a week."

Marcelle laughed. "Don't you get used to it up here. You going to be back down there with all of them soon enough. Only this time you going to know how to handle it."

"How? How?" I spun away from the window, imploring her to tell me fast and loud.

"God!" she sang. "Jesus!"—fast, loud, wrong.

"Oh," I said, making little attempt to mask my dissatisfaction with her answer. "Him." She might as well have given me a hand-knit aubergine and pink scarf for all the good it did me.

"Yes, him. He's going to help you."

"Great."

I slouched back to bed. She knew not to talk about it anymore and entertained me, instead, with tales of her adolescence in the south and how she had been married to a man named Garfield, but that he had drowned in a fishing accident. Her eyes never once teared over, even as mine cried buckets. The doctor who came to take a blood sample gave me a quizzical look and Marcelle made herself interested in her knitting.

When he left, she looked at her watch. "We gotta get you some breakfast. It ought to have been here by now. You skinny enough as it is."

"I look skinny to you?"

"Well, in all honesty, I can't tell. You lyin' flat on your back in a bed, after all. And if it's so, I ain't sayin' it's a good thing. You white girls take skinny as a compliment. That's funny. Even the word, the way it sound, makes it pretty plain it ain't an attribute to be encouraged. Skinny as a snake. You not a snake." She eyed me, as if I might be.

"No, I'm not a snake. I'm a cat."

"A cat!" she beamed. Folding up her knitting, she placed herself plump on the side of my bed and started to pet my hair. "You is a little cat." I curled and wriggled at the soft touch of her rough hand. I was glad I was there with her. I was glad I had done what I did if it meant that I could lie in a slim white bed and have a large black lady stroke my cheek.

She moved her chair so that it was next to my bed, in order to underline the fact that she would no longer be watching me, but that for the rest of my stay she would be *being* with me. I asked her, later, as I ate my lunch, whether she was this nice to everyone she was assigned to watch.

"First off, I take assignations from no one but the Lord. Second, I'm cordial to everyone, but nice to the people I think are nice in their bellies . . ."

"Nice in their bellies or nice in their hearts?"

"Down in their bellies, because the heart can be worked on with music, film, and books."

"That's true, for sure. What's wrong with that?"

"Your belly be the only organ you cannot fool."

Agreeing wholeheartedly, I stuffed it full of Jell-O, a truthful dessert if ever there was one, and waited for my next blood test. Soon enough, the results were back and the doctor announced that I was all clear.

"No liver damage. We'll let you go around lunchtime tomorrow."

Forty

I used to be frightened of flowers

There was a knock at the door and Rachel came striding in to see me, bearing flowers in tones of purple and red, royalty and blood. "Thank you," I nodded, as she bent to kiss my cheek. She was wearing high-heeled sandals made of snakeskin. Through the open toes, her nails shimmied in their pearlescent pedicure. The nail on one of her big toes was in a better condition than my entire life.

She shook her head. "Really, Ruby. This is not," she said, motioning to the hospital bed, "the best way to begin a friendship."

I stretched my arms above my head, coquettish, ridiculous in my hospital smock. "You want to be my friend?"

"Of course I do."

"I wasn't sure."

She changed the subject. "Scott is very upset. He wanted to fly in and see you, but I stopped him."

"Thank you. You did the right thing."

"I always do the right thing."

"No. You let me into your house. I think, perhaps, that that was wrong."

"Maybe. I don't think so."

"Thank you for the flowers."

"I'm glad you like them."

"I don't really!" I laughed, hoarse. "I like them because they're from you. But, to be honest, flowers have always kind of scared me. I worry about the bugs they could be hiding."

She ran her manicured hand across the heads of the flowers, which rubbed themselves against her touch. "See, nothing nestling in here. Except the very best wishes for the very best girl. Is there something I should have brought you instead? Chocolates? Fruit?"

"Nah. I don't really feel like eating. I figure this, all this, can at least be utilized as a successful diet. Fuck Dr. Atkins. Screw Weight Watchers. If a person is serious about losing weight, they should prove it by trying to kill themselves. And if they survive, then they deserve to be thin. And their hospital recuperation period will play host to a transformation."

"Very good, Ruby. Shut the fuck up." She kissed my forehead. "I'm glad that you're still on the planet."

The phone rang. It was Sean. At first I couldn't place him, without his big head in front of me. He was so excited that he forgot, for a few minutes, where it was he was calling me.

"Ruby! Great news!"

"About my suicide attempt?"

"Oh, shit. Oh, yeah right." He paused to think of an inspiring piece of wisdom to impart but then decided against it. "Listen, you crazy bitch."

"I'm listening," I said.

"There's bidding war for *Mean People Suck*. I screened a cut on Sunday and Lions Gate made an offer right away. Then Miramax got wind of it, right, but then Sony Pictures Classics offered more. Things are looking great. And you know what else? It's you that hooked them. They're all saying that it's the best performance by a young actress since Jodie Foster in *Taxi Driver*."

"Fuck off."

"No joke."

"Does that mean you're the new Scorsese?"

"It means that I already have financing for my next film. I'm writing it for you."

"I don't know that I can go through all this again."

"It's a comedy."

"Can we talk about this when I get out?"

"Yeah, sure." A baby started to gurgle in the background. "So, Ruby, I just wanted to say thank you."

Rachel leaned over and kissed me on the forehead.

"No problem," I said, waving goodbye to her as she left.

Forty-one

Time to get up now

Marcelle brought my dinner on a tray without a word, then went back to her chair and her gaze, which I followed out above the traffic to the movie theater on Greenwich Avenue.

Looking at the theater, I suddenly had the desire to leave my cozy bed and my soothing babysitter. I wanted to get out. I wanted to be alive, in the world. I wanted to pay to see things, pay to hear things, and pay to read things. I wanted to pay to wear things on my body, which had, I couldn't help but note, morphed into a more pleasing shape in the time I had been away from the world.

As the sun set over Manhattan, in a stream of orange and navy, Marcelle clicked out of her silent reverie and back into language.

"Ohmigod. God is love. It is so wonderful to know him. He is with me every minute of the day, talking to me, listening to me."

"That sounds lovely, Marcelle."

"It is the most beautiful thing. And it is the most normal thing too, for he never leaves my side. Sometime I don't even realize he is there, because he is so quiet, looking after me."

I guess it doesn't make a lot of noise to look after someone. I guess you just make noise when you need looking after. I liked her description of this quiet man who supported her in every way. Head melting into the pillow as sleep began to caress my face, I asked, "Does He always forgive you?"

"Yes! I'm forgiven a thousand times. And so are you! That is why you is sitting here, talking to me right now. Because you are forgiven. It is going to be all right. It is going to be fine, because He saved you. He got a special plan for you."

She closed her eyes in ecstasy and sang out loud, "Jesus loves you!"

Thank you. Thank you, Jesus. I did not love him back, not at all, but I was so grateful for His love. I will always remember Marcelle as the first and last person who made me believe in God. For a few short hours I was a devout believer. But I think it was really her I believed in. When she left during the night, my belief was gone too. I woke up in the morning, an atheist again. Between my sleep and waking, I saw someone I did believe in.

Forty-two

You again?

Her eyes sprang open and she knew enough, instinctively, to shut them tight again. There was a stirring in the corner of the room. Ruby was frightened, the first time she had felt the rapid car-alarm heartbeat since she had tried to dull it altogether. Peering under her lashes, she watched a shadowy figure leaning against the window, staring out into the night.

"Marcelle?" she asked foolishly, for she knew it was not her.

Again, hopeful, like opening the fridge only five minutes after you last looked, "Marcelle, is that you?"

When no answer came, she closed her eyes again, gripping the sheets. "Just because I tried to kill myself, Lord," she prayed, "does not mean I want to die." A heavy footstep toward her bed, then another, then more. In five steps, she knew he was beside her. Tasting blood on her tongue as she bit into her lip, she opened her eyes, wide as she could, attempting to convey courage, feeling none at all.

191

A man, maybe six feet tall, maybe dark, maybe foreign, maybe a man.

"Ruby?"

The blood from her lip trickled down her chin, the metallic taste mixing with the fear on her tongue.

"Ruby, is that you?"

She raised her hand from her side and brought it slowly to her mouth. With the back of her hand, she tried to wipe the blood away, but managed only to streak it across her cheek, onto her neck, and back down to the white hospital sheet. It was more blood than a lip ought to contain and she wondered if perhaps it were fake and she were being filmed, her terrorizer and extra hired by Sean to get a true reaction.

"Do I know you?"

"You did once. I doubt you would remember me. I used to be a friend of your family. I lodged in your house for a few months."

Ruby gasped, a rivulet of blood passing back into her throat so that she almost gagged. This was not how it was supposed to be. He was never meant to see her like this. Or maybe he was? Maybe that was the whole point of the past week. That this was the only way to see him again. Not certain how to proceed, she leaned over to the night table and gargled with the water in the plastic cup.

Holding the water in her mouth, she eased herself out of bed and went to the bathroom where she spat into the sink. Wiping her face with a wet paper towel, she looked for the answer in the mirror, as she always did. As ever, the answer did not come. She padded past him without a glance, and hauled herself back into bed. Fluffing her two sad pillows as best she could, she leaned back, ready to talk.

"I think I know who you are." She did not want to say it aloud in case the words chased him away. He did not want the words said in case they obliged him to leave. Her own Scottish Play, bad luck after all? And all this time she had imagined him her good-luck charm. He was heavier. The thick hair had continued to sprout, in new, uncalled-for places: his nostrils, the nape of his neck, his ears. He had a black and white beard, neatly trimmed, and his mouth sat like a red interloper inside it.

The Star of David was no longer around his neck. In its place were a couple of hippyish beads on a beige leather string. His flannel shirt was undone several buttons from the top down and two from the bottom up. It was too heavy for the summer heat. She thought, perhaps, he was hiding a messy body. Then she wondered what he was thinking about her body, her face, her hair? As though he could hear her thoughts and was determined to be truthful, Liev, because it was Liev, not ghost of Liev or son of Liev, announced, "Your skin is green."

"Greenish. It's the pills. Not fabulous for the complexion. Sorry."

"I didn't say that you looked bad. I think you look beautiful. It's just that, right now, you are beautiful in the key of green."

She thought about how many times she had heard the word "beautiful" since she had been in the hospital and how many times she had heard it in the last year, how many times in her life. How often had she thought of the word without saying it out loud. And if you think such a word, but don't expel it with your voice, does it turn to poison in your brain?

Her thoughts began to swim, struggling against the waves in the room, falling now and then, beneath the waves completely.

"I don't know," she shook her head vigorously, "I don't know if I'm still me. I'm not sure that you're you."

"Do you believe I was there all those years ago?"

"Yes. Of course you were there."

He watched her with brown eyes, the depth of the darkness in them sucking out the phosphorous overhead light in the bathroom. It blew out, silently. He was, in the darkness, a man in the shape of a man. She was a girl in the shape of a girl, beneath her sharp starched sheets.

"I am here now."

"How do I know it's you?" she queried, stern as a schoolteacher.

"How do I know it's you, Ruby?" he answered, with the flip drawl of a schoolboy who knows that Miss has a loveless home life.

"Of course it's me. I look the same."

"No you don't." He edged toward the foot of the bed, where he laid his fingers on the sheet that encased her toes. He traced the sheet upward, as she lay, still as a mummy, eyes darting furiously in the dark.

"You didn't have hips before," he journeyed gently up the bed. "You didn't have breasts before."

Her eyes came to rest as she asked, tremulous, "Now that I do, I suppose you don't love me anymore."

Still gentle, not looking up, he moved his hand away and walked back toward the window. Talking to New York, he told the city, and its one other inhabitant, "I'm not a fucking pedophile. I loved you because you were you. You don't think it destroyed me that you were a little girl?" He traced the New York skyline on the window with his finger. "Do you know where I've been for all this time?"

He waited for New York to answer, but Ruby piped up, instead: "No. I have wondered every night. It's been the first thing I've asked myself every morning. It's what I always thought about during sex with Scott or lovemaking with Sebastian. I used the thought as others count sheep, only it didn't soothe me. Where have you been?"

He looked sideways at her. "Do you remember when you looked up at me and said, 'Baby, I wanna fuck'?"

It sounded far more shocking coming out of his mouth than it had from hers as a little girl. She covered her ears but it didn't stop her hearing him when he whispered, "I was inside the answer."

"What are you talking about?" she hissed, moving her hands to cover her mouth, her words unmuffled by them.

He pulled a red pen from his pocket and drew her mouth over the back of her palm, pulling back as he spoke to admire his work.

"When you said that to me, you trapped me inside a sheet of glass. That's what happens when a little girl says 'fuck' and knows what it means."

She moved her hands, and her mouth, flesh and blood beneath them, was tinged blue. "My mother told me what it meant. Years before I met you."

He sat down against the wall, legs crossed in lotus position, and tilted his head back. "You sort of look like Lila, you know." Liev stared at her until she had to look away. When she looked back, he was gazing at the skyline.

Irritated by mention of his ex-girlfriend now as she had been then, she turned on her side, so they were both looking out the window. She tried to look at the same thing as him, but it was difficult to pinpoint in the dark. His voice trailed again, like a velvet ribbon rolled out from the corner.

"You never met Lila, I don't think. But she had watched you sleep one night, after a dinner party at your parents' house, before I was there. I told her how I felt about you and she said that she had only glanced at you, but she thought she understood. Lila's dead now. She was strangled in the shower by a homeless artist she took home one night."

"My father didn't tell me. We don't speak. I'm so sorry. You must really miss her."

"I miss a lot of people."

She felt the velvet ribbon real and rubbed it against her nose. "Me too."

She thought she could hear him smile. He felt his lips ease back over his teeth as if this were the first time. It hurt. He rubbed his teeth with his thumb and wondered whether or not he should show her. Since there was very little either of them could see, this far away from each other, he decided he would tell her about it.

Forty-three

Going-home present

"I have a drawing for you. I've kept it with me," he paused as he put his hand in the pocket of his flannel shirt, "just in case we ever ran into each other again. It think it is my finest work."

He popped open his wallet. It was thick with bills, which he pulled out one by one. They looked like dollars, but some of them had pictures of her mother on them where Hamilton should have been. With the last one laid out on the floor, he unfolded, from miniature, a scrap of lined paper just under 8½ x 11. It was ripped from a scratch pad of low quality, a ninety-nine-cent bodega job. Moving back toward the bed as though on wheels, he placed the picture in her hand.

"I drew it on a plane back from home a few summers ago. First I drew my tray of airplane food, beaten and bruised in its plastic coffin. Then I drew the view from the window, clouds and clouds and clouds, and who cares for clouds when they aren't lying on their backs? Then the man with the headphones, sleeping beside me, the deep, clean sleep of the dull. I had more success drawing the miniature bottles of wine on his tray. Things in miniature tend to be pretty convincing, whether they are children or bottles of alcohol, don't you think?"

She didn't answer. Leaning across the bed, to the lamp on the side table, she brought white back into the room. Sitting up straight, she pulled her hair out of her face and saw the other face on the lined notepaper. Ruby looked at the little girl, rendered in pen strokes of love and defeat, the girl's eyes huge with playful questioning, the artist's strokes small with answers unspeakable.

"How did you remember how I looked, Liev?"

"I don't know that I did. I remembered you, that's true. But I'm not sure you did look like that. All these years, I wanted you to check for yourself. Did you look like that, Ruby?"

She followed the sweeps of the pen. The ink was so solemn, and yet the girl inside the troubled black ink was not troubled at all, but mischievous and excited.

"Yes. I think I did look like that."

He leaned over the bed and she steeled herself not to flinch when he kissed her forehead. His beard felt smooth, the cartoon beard of a kindly grandfather. She touched it and it grew in her hand, curls wrapping themselves round her fingers. He smelled of clean-cut grass, mixed with a pinch of the other kind of grass, more heady, not unpleasant, although the connotations were of Aslan and other little boys she had encountered on the Lower East Side. Both scents were glaringly inappropriate in the hospital, the former making a mockery of all the "fresh scent" disinfectants splashed along the hallways. The latter just making a mockery.

"What are you doing here, Liev?"

He shrugged his shoulders and the curls snapped back. "I have been assigned to watch you."

"You always were," she thought.

"I really missed you," he said, . . . no longer able to fake indifference.

She almost laughed. "I really missed you" made him sound like a school friend reconnected with after a summer camp apart. She did not know what to say. She was trying not to breathe too hard.

He lay beside her. She sobbed, as ever, but the tears did not leave the ducts and the ducts began to multiply under her skin, until they were lining every vein and string of flesh inside her. They formed, twofold, along the wall of her uterus and down along her vaginal passage. They covered the darkness that Aslan had discovered, but that Sebastian had chosen to ignore, and the darkness turned, not to light, but to sweet pink, sad tears, spread out, turned juicy, happy, sensual.

She knew a doctor would be back to check on her soon. Inspired by relief, she moved his hand to her mouth, to her breast, between her legs and then she reached up under his flannel shirt and unbuckled his belt, touching him as he touched her. It was done in under a minute, but she kept his hand under her hospital gown, holding it in protective place with her own. He was gasping now, harder than she had been, and she tried to shush him. He snatched his hand away and leaped across the room.

"What have I done? What have I just done? I'm sorry, I'm so sorry. Please don't tell your father."

"I don't talk to my father anymore. And besides, I'm twenty years old, you understand that, no?"

"No."

He went to the bathroom to wash his hands. There he took a few deep breaths, looking at his reflection in the mirror, where hers had been a few minutes earlier. Ruby's face was still there, just under his own. It floated to the surface within a few seconds and, screwing up his eyes, he ducked his whole skull under the cold faucet.

"I'm going to have a bath," said Ruby, head bowed in mock shame.

"Of course. Just leave the door open."

Ruby inched the taps into action, opening the hot tank wide. Presently, she dipped her toe into the water and, finding it just this side of bearable, stepped into the tub, where she sat with her knees up by her chin. Captain of a synchronized swimming team consisting of one, she suddenly kicked her legs up into the air and let her torso fall back into the water until her hair was submerged, but her face hovered prettily above the water level. Then her arms stretched back behind her head, her hands resting on the rim of the tub, her toes on its southern counterpart. Arching her hip she raised her tummy up into the air. It glistened, rounded, like the body of a pre-pubescent child.

She stayed that way as long as she could hold it and then flipped onto her tummy. Taking a deep breath, she ducked her face beneath the surface. She felt her newly grown-in hair take flight on the water, just long enough to float behind her pale neck like a fashion accessory. Beneath the water, she blew out bubbles. In one bubble was Rachel, dressed in pink, like Glinda the Good Witch. When Rachel had floated so far into the distance that she could no longer be discerned by the naked eye, Ruby came back up for air. She shook her wet hair, splashing water across the room, and then stepped, neatly, precisely and purposefully, out of the bath. No one was there to hand her a towel. She handed herself her own towel and went back outside.

She imagined what she had gone through since she was a kid, experienced by a grown-up man about to hit middle age. She felt suddenly sickened by him and envisioned, in a flash, all the people who had felt sickened by her.

Aware that she was thinking deep thoughts, but unsure what they were, he guessed quick and wrong. "We could try to make this work, Ruby. When you get out of here."

She imagined Liev brushing his teeth, the two shiny front teeth that rested on his wet lip coated in Colgate. She imagined him pissing in the toilet bowl. Well, yes, she had touched his cock, with her hands when it was hard. But to look at it when it was soft. How could she not laugh? She never wanted to laugh at him or be embarrassed by his body.

And even if they didn't live together, what were she and Liev going to do? Go out on dates? Have dinners together, intimate candlelight suppers? Go to the roller rink? Decide whether or not they liked each other enough to "go all the way?" She was here, now, a grown-up more childish but less childlike than she was when he knew her. If she let him get to know her, then what? Well, then what? Just because she knew, when it was over, that she did not want him, didn't mean she didn't want him to want her as much as he ever had. As much as she had imagined he had.

"You think that we would stand a chance in the real world?"

"How do you know I'm talking about the real world? You don't know where I've been. You don't know the places I could take you to see if this could work. Reality doesn't have to come into it. You could keep me inside your head, where I've always been, only this time you would be in my head too."

"I don't know what you mean . . ."

"You wouldn't have to know. You would just have to trust me. Do you think you could do that?"

"Liev, for the longest time you were the only person I could trust. Which makes no sense at all, I know, because you weren't even there. But whenever I felt someone did me wrong, whenever I felt mistreated, I imagined you telling them off, leaping to my defense. Would I have been right?"

"Of course you would. You think this was about sex, don't you? The reason I was trapped behind glass?"

"I . . . children are very sexual. There's nothing more sexual than a twelve-year-old girl."

"That wasn't what I wanted. That's not what I was afraid of. There's something in my life that's a lot bigger than sex. Honestly, I don't do sex at all."

She wondered if it was a drug he had given up or a drug he had never been interested in. "This isn't going to be about God again, is it? Because I've been hearing a lot about Jesus Christ and his old man lately. If you're going to talk about Jesus I'm going to have to say to you what I said to Marcelle and to that awful nun . . ."

"No, not God."

"Oh, fuck. Not heroin? Is that why you were always indoors?"

"No," he laughed, "not heroin."

"Then what?"

"Do you trust me?"

"You and me alone in this room right now? Yes, I trust you."

"Good. Because right now is all we have going for us. You and I don't exist beyond this room. I don't know how you got into the situation that led you to this hospital bed. But I think I can give you a fresh start so that never come back."

"Oh, you can, can you?" She cocked an eyebrow at him.

"Don't be coy with me. You don't have to do that. Just be yourself."

Smarting at his jibe, she turned her face away. "I can't remember how to do that."

"That's why I'm going to help you."

"And you don't want to have sex with me?"

"No. I guess . . . if that were an option for me then, yes, of course I would want to make love to you. This penetration you people have such a fixation on, if you wanted me to do that, I would."

"What people? Liev, it's not a new practice."

Liev shook his head at her vulgarity. Then he unbuttoned his shirt and took it off, laying it on the chair. His body was not messy, as she had expected. It was not as she had expected at all. Broad and sinewy, his chest was so pale that, between patches of fur, she could see the veins beneath the skin. And within those veins she could clearly see the ebb and flow of blood, rich purple-red. He crawled onto her bed. He pulled himself on top of her, and turned her head to the side. The cut on her neck was still there. With a pointed tongue he licked the scratch, following it from beginning to end as she looked to the door for advice, desperate for a doctor or nurse to pass by. He bit down and she was not fearful anymore. The pain was little; his teeth on her neck felt like two tiny rabbit punches.

Then ruby was everywhere. Then ruby was gone. Then ruby was clean. Then Ruby was saved.

"Mommy," she whimpered.

Her childhood friend asked a question, the words coated in blood. "Do you think that you can let me go in the morning?"

"Yes," she answered, her voice steady now, "I think so."

Forty-four

Stick a fork in me, I'm done

The sun baked through the window and her first thought, on waking, was whether or not she was cooked yet. A doctor was taking blood from her arm in a syringe that caught the light like a spinning top. She watched the silver retract and the red it took with it, terribly suave and persuasive, as Ruby pleaded, "Don't go. I need you here with me."

"I think something happened in the night," said Ruby to the doctor. "I think he's gone."

"Who's gone?'

"The man who you had watching me."

"There was no man, Ruby. I don't think that Sister Ann would appreciate that insult one little bit. She was watching you again last night. She said she had so enjoyed your conversation about religion the other day, she requested to watch you again. She said you slept sound as a baby. I must say, you are looking so much better than when you came in here. Look at your arms."

She looked at her arms, as instructed, but there was nothing there to see. Skin, but nothing on the skin. Nothing etched on it or cut from it. The silver syringe had dug its national flag in an expanse of pure white.

Forty-five

Flowers

The twins picked me up. Red twin cried and smothered my face with kisses. But yellow twin just shook her head and muttered, "You're dumb," as though I had tipped a rude waitress too much money. "Let's get ice cream," she added and red twin immediately dried her tears and perked up. "YEAH!" she honked. "Pistachio!"

"YEAH," squawked yellow twin, "kids who have just tried to kill themselves should eat a lot of pistachio!"

"But I want macadamia," I pleaded as I pulled my dress over my head.

"No," snapped yellow, as she buckled my shoe, "that's only for people recovering from accidents with kitchen utensils."

Forty-six

The start

The day I got out of hospital the Gay Pride Parade was slithering across the West Village like a bedazzled snake. As I swung through the revolving doors, "Some WHERE over the rainbow!" played from a sound system. I blocked my ears, because I'd just come back from there and it hadn't been at all as I'd expected.

The magic slippers were a half-size too small. The lollipops the little people handed me tasted of oral sex with a pervert. Halfway down the yellow brick road a cop pulled out from nowhere and ticketed me for speeding. I kept running into tiny actresses with huge eyes and bigger voices, hooked on speed, begetting other actresses with huge eyes and bigger voices hooked on speed, like a Golden Age of Hollywood hall of mirrors. And the only wicked witch I ever got to throw water on was myself. Flying monkeys—lovers stalked and spurned—cackled as I melted into a waxy green puddle on the floor. But by then I was too tired to care. I decided it was okay to melt if it meant that I didn't have to be the villain anymore.

Fingers in my ears, I surveyed the variety of banners being waved from the passing floats: "Coalition of Gay Latinos," "Association of Leather Slaves," "Female to Male Transgender Society." It reminded me of the video store four blocks west of my apartment, where the sci-fi section is not listed in alphabetical order, but contains a zillion subsections, including "Cyber-Punk," "Time Travel" and "Dystopia." I think the theory is, if you keep dividing and subdividing a group, eventually the group is one—you and you alone. Then you have a name, your true name to describe what you are.

I don't believe, nowadays, that Ruby is such a bad description. There are connotations of blood, but also of oranges, the vanity of lipstick, and the many-faceted translucence of the stone itself. Hold me up to the light in order that you might truly see who I am. In the dark, I'm not really me. This is how it will be. I made myself melt and now I get to reconfigure myself as I choose: girl born, not from mother or father, not from nature or nurture, not from a lover who treated her badly or a lover who treated her well. Girl born of the girl herself. Once you have made yourself ugly, succeeded in your harebrained mission beyond your wildest dreams, there is nothing left to do but become beautiful again.

As many as one in three
Americans with HIV...
DO NOT KNOW IT.

More than half of those
who will get HIV this year...
ARE UNDER 25.

HIV is preventable.
You can help fight AIDS.
Get informed. Get the facts.

www.knowhivaids.org
1-866-344-KNOW